# GASPARILLA'S TREASURE

## SCOTT CLEMENTS

Gasparilla's Treasure
by Scott Clements

First Printing, 2012

ISBN 978-1475028539

To everyone who sees life as an adventure.

## PROLOGUE

December – 1821

Darkness overtook Gasparilla as he plummeted deeper into the murky ocean. A massive storm raged as cannon fire tore through his ship. Just moments before, Gasparilla had wrapped himself in the ship's heavy anchor chains as lightning ripped across the sky, silhouetting him against the blackness of night.

He roared above the cannon fire and cracks of thunder, "Gasparilla dies by his own hand, no one else's!" He released the ship's anchor, the weight pulling him into the hungry depths of the Gulf of Mexico.

Clutched in his hand was his most treasured possession. He had heard his men call it *The Staff of Gasparilla*, and he liked that name. At first glance, it appeared to be a simple walking stick, but what made it extraordinary was the handle. It was called *Arbol de la Lechuza,* and was carved from a single diamond that was about the size of Gasparilla's fist.

Fate had delivered *Arbol de la Lechuza* to him during his first battle as a pirate captain. Gasparilla and his crew attacked a Spanish treasure ship that carried a year's worth of riches from the new world to King Charles III. The battle was not going well for Gasparilla. He was about to lose everything: this battle, his ship, his men, and his life.

In a desperate move, Gasparilla boarded the Spanish ship and fought his way to the cargo hold. He refused to end his career without touching a single piece of treasure.

When he reached it, the cargo hold was full of gold coins, ornate weapons, and other elaborate treasures, but Gasparilla only saw *Arbol de la Lechuza*. The moment he held it, he could feel his luck had changed.

*Arbol de la Lechuza* was incredibly detailed. The base was a tree trunk with the hint of an old wise man's face twisted in its curves. From the trunk grew the gnarled branches that wove their way in and out of each other to form a hollow sphere. Tiny leaves hung from each branch, and if you looked closely, you could see delicate veins running through the leaves. In the middle of the sphere sat a miniature owl, perfect in every detail. The owl was no more than an inch tall, but every feather appeared real.

No one knew the age or origin of Arbol de la Lechuza, but Gasparilla knew one thing from his own experience: It had strange, unexplainable powers. It also carried with it the legend that it would one day choose its true master. And that person would have unimaginable power.

Gasparilla's lungs ached as he wiggled his arm free of the ship's binding chains at the bottom of the Gulf of Mexico. Every cell of his body cried out for oxygen. As his consciousness slowly slipped away, he raised his hand in front of his face and a sliver of moonlight filtered down through the murky depths. He could just discern the outline of the object he grasped tightly in front of his face. The Staff of Gasparilla. The desire for oxygen was too strong. He drew a deep breath of cold, salty death.

## CHAPTER ONE

With a bounce in his step, thirteen-year-old Trip Montgomery paraded through the halls of *The Good Ole' Times* retirement community, oozing confidence. Every day at six thirty, Trip brought dinner to his great-grandfather, Pappy. Despite the age of the average resident, Trip didn't appear out of place there.

He was a good-looking kid with a smile that stretched from ear to ear. Most of Trip's friends found it difficult to understand how he could go there every day. The idea of being around that many old people just gave them the creeps; but that wasn't the case for Trip. He liked his visits to *Good Ole' Times,* mostly because he enjoyed seeing Pappy. But he also got a great deal of satisfaction from bringing smiles to the faces of the residents. As he strolled through the common area where the residents played cards, dominoes, and worked on puzzles, Trip always took a moment to say hello.

"Hey Miss Helen, that sure is a beautiful dress you're wearing," Trip called out as he sauntered passed. Flustered, Miss Helen dropped one of her dominoes with a clatter. Trip spotted Mr. Brown seated in a comfortable, overstuffed chair reading a book.

"Mr. Brown. I'm not letting you out of that arm wrestling rematch. I'm still convinced you found a way to cheat," teased Trip, as he gave the old man a wink. He and Mr. Brown had a best two out of three arm wrestling match a few weeks back. Trip could have easily won. He was healthy, strong, and excelled at sports, but he thought Mr. Brown would enjoy a victory. And Trip was right. Even now, at the mere mention of it, a big smile crept across Mr. Brown's lips. As Trip continued across the room, he spotted Mr. Anderson.

"Now you take it easy on her, Mr. Anderson," warned Trip. "You know she doesn't see all that well." Mr. Anderson looked up from his fan of cards, happy to see Trip.

"Hey! Good to see you, Trip," said Mr. Anderson warmly. "How's your Pappy doing? I haven't seen him for a few days."

"We'll see. I hope it's a good day," replied Trip.

"Well you make sure to tell him hello for me. Even if he doesn't remember who I am," said Mr. Anderson.

That stopped Trip for a moment. Pappy and Mr. Anderson had been good friends for a while, but Pappy's mind was not quite right any more. It troubled Trip that Pappy could forget a friend like Mr. Anderson. When Trip tried to discuss it with his mom, she would say something like, *it's tough getting old*, or *these things happen*.

It seemed to Trip that Pappy was drifting further and further from reality. How long had it been since Pappy remembered who Trip was? Weeks? Maybe a month? Even on the days when Pappy didn't remember Trip, it was still fun. Pappy usually had some crazy adventure he was reenacting. But some days he would just sit there staring out the window with a blank, sad look on his face. There was nothing Trip could do on those days to lighten Pappy's mood.

But the days Trip enjoyed most, were the days when Pappy would tell him stories of his childhood adventures; the real stories, not the stories of his fantasies.

Just last week, Trip was telling Pappy about Eli, the kid who was bullying him at school, and Pappy responded with a story about the bullies that used to call him names and chase him through the streets of St. Augustine, shoes clattering on the cobblestone roads.

Pappy was about the same age as Trip at the time, and the bullies pursued him through the city and on to the hot sands of the beach. Pappy ran full out, afraid for his life. He paused for a breather and frantically looked around for a good hiding spot, when something glinted and caught his eye.

It sparkled in the sunlight; half buried in the beach sand near a palm tree. He knew he needed to keep running, but his curiosity got the best of him and he stopped to check it out. He was glad he took the time to investigate.

As he got close to the shining object, Pappy felt it had a *magical* quality, like it was calling out to him. He gently brushed the sand away and carefully picked it up. Serenity spread over him and his breath slowed. He could barely move.

It was a small piece of iron with a jewel embedded in it. He held the jewel in his outstretched hand as the bullies closed in. Pappy was mesmerized, unable to run away.

The bullies walked right up to the spot where he stood. It was as if they did not see him at all. They stood not more than two feet away, but did nothing. Pappy looked at the jewel, and then back to the bullies as a smile stretched across his face. It was precisely at that moment that the biggest bully landed a knock out blow, hard, to the center of Pappy's nose.

When Pappy told Trip stories like this, he knew he could deal with his own problems.

Trip arrived at Pappy's door and took a deep breath.

"Please let it be a good day," he whispered to himself as he grabbed the doorknob. With another deep breath, he turned the knob and went in.

Pappy balanced precariously on a chair and waved his arms wildly in the air as if swatting at invisible bugs swarming around his head. He was full of energy and looked like he was having a great time. Trip smiled at the sight of it. If there was not going to be any interesting conversation  today, at least it would still be entertaining.

"Come on Pappy. Get down from there and have something to eat. There will be time for that later," coaxed Trip with a chuckle.

"I was just trying to get rid of these pesky bats!" explained Pappy as he climbed off the chair.

"Do you remember who I am today, Pappy?" Trip asked hopefully.

"Of course I do. Do you think I'm crazy or something?" replied Pappy, offended.

"Oh good, because I was hoping to get some advice on a few things," said Trip.

"In due time, General Shakelston. But first I need to ask you a question," said Pappy.

"General Shakelston?"

"Yes, you are General Earl Shakelston, U.S. Army," replied Pappy. "But what I can't figure out is, why a man of your rank is bringing me my food?"

For a moment, Trip felt let down. He had hoped Pappy would be able to have a real conversation. But Trip realized those were selfish feelings. He was here for Pappy, not for himself.

Trip whispered to himself, "It's OK, Pappy. Maybe you'll remember tomorrow." And then he put on his best performance, "Well, General Montgomery. We have some serious strategies to discuss and I feel it's best if we have a little dinner and then..."

Pappy reached out and grabbed Trip's arm, stopping Trip in mid sentence. Trip looked into Pappy's eyes and saw them filled with an intensity and focus he had never seen before. Was this part of Pappy's delusion? It couldn't be. Pappy looked as if he were present one hundred percent. Even on good days, Pappy still had a dreamy look in his eyes, as if he only allowed a certain percentage of his attention to come back to reality. But every bit of Pappy's attention was here, right now, in this reality.

"Trip. Listen carefully!" said Pappy intently. "I need you to do something for me. There's a trunk in the attic of your house. It's important. You need to find that trunk... Your father..." Pappy found it difficult to keep his tentative grip on reality. He struggled, but tried to continue, "Your father and I... You're the last hope. There's no more money... don't you see? I'll die!"

Trip started to worry. Pappy never talked about dying before. In all the time they had spent together, Pappy never behaved like this.

"What's going on, Pappy? Let me get the nurse!" said Trip, worried.

"No, Trip!" pleaded Pappy. "You have to do this for me. Can't you see? There's no other way!" Pappy's eyes filled with tears. Now Trip was really concerned. He needed to get some help.

"That's enough!" said Trip sternly. "I'm getting the nurse now." But Pappy's grip tightened on Trip's arm.

15

Pappy continued desperately, "There's no way your mom can take care of me. They're going to kick me out of this place. She can't afford to keep me in here any more. It's the only way! Promise me you'll do it. Get that trunk! Promise me!"

Trip was confused, and not exactly sure what Pappy wanted from him, but he knew Pappy really meant it.

"Yeah, sure, Pappy," soothed Trip. "I'll get the trunk. But what exactly is in it? What do you want me to do with it?"

"I said promise me!" begged Pappy. "You have to promise me, now!"

"Of course! I promise. I promise," said Trip hastily. "Now what is in the trunk? What do you want me to do with it?"

Pappy allowed his delusion to take him back away from reality.

"General Shakelston," said Pappy. "You are speaking nonsense. Here we are discussing military strategy and suddenly you start asking about some trunk. Have you gone mad?"

Trip was too shaken up to dive back into the fantasy, "Sorry General Mongomery," said Trip. "I will try to pay more attention."

But there was no way Trip could pay attention to this role-play any more. What just happened here? Pappy insisted this trunk was in Mom's attic, and said if Trip did not find it, he would die. Did Pappy believe the trunk had magical powers to keep him alive? No, he said they needed money, money to keep Pappy here in the retirement home. Maybe the trunk contained savings bonds or stocks, or something even more valuable. But why wouldn't he just tell Mom to get the trunk?

There were so many questions, but Trip knew a couple of things for sure. First, there was no way he could let Pappy die. Second, even if Pappy was crazy and that trunk had nothing to do with whether he lived or died, it was important to Pappy that he find that trunk. And finally, if Pappy wanted Trip to find it, he would find it.

## CHAPTER TWO

When Trip got home, he still could not make sense of what Pappy had told him. He was sure Mom would be able to help him understand.

Trip's dad died eight years ago when Trip was just five years old. Mom would never really tell Trip what happened, and any time Trip brought it up, she would tell him about how much his father loved him or how proud he would have been of Trip. One thing Trip did know was that his father's death was unexpected, and they were left with very little money. They had Pappy's retirement, but it wasn't enough, so Mom started giving private music lessons to make ends meet.

Halfway through dinner, Mom's reaction was surprising Trip. She was always very interested to hear about Pappy, especially when he had been more or less himself. But this conversation was not going well at all.

"You can't believe anything your Pappy says Trip," argued Mom. "He's delusional."

"I'm tellin' you, Mom," insisted Trip. "I haven't seen him this focused in years. He really knew who I was and what he was saying. I've never seen him that way before. He was dead serious, and he made me promise."

"Even if all of that is true, which I'm sure it's not," admonished Mom, "I don't want to hear another word about this trunk. OK?"

"But Mom, he told me…"

"No! It stops here!" interrupted Mom. "That trunk has already caused too many problems!" Those words hung in the air. Trip thought about what she had just said. The trunk caused problems.

"So there *is* a trunk," said Trip.

Mom knew she was caught. Once the words were out there, she could not take them back. Trip was too smart for that.

"OK fine," admitted Mom. "There is a trunk. But I will not let you waste away your life like both your great grandfather and your father did. And that is final!"

"You mean Dad knew about this trunk too?" asked Trip, the excitement growing in his voice. "This is huge!"

Mom had worked herself into a corner. She had no choice. "Your father wouldn't stop obsessing over that ridiculous trunk. Every spare minute, he and Pappy would be up in the attic tinkering with that thing."

She saw the look on Trip's face and stopped him before he could say anything.

"Don't even ask," said Mom. "I don't know anything, they wouldn't tell me. But every few months Pappy and Dad would get a wild hair and be off on some wild goose chase. They wouldn't tell me what they were doing, or where they were going, but I know it had to do with that trunk."

Trip could see this conversation had really affected Mom. She stared down at her plate, absentmindedly playing with what was left of her dinner. Mom had given him a lot of information, and Trip needed a little time to take it all in.

It was bedtime, and Trip just finished brushing his teeth. He wanted to write down a few of the things he learned today before he forgot. He was on his way to the desk to grab paper and pen when he noticed Mom sitting at a table pouring over some bills. She did not look happy.

"Is everything OK, Mom?" Trip asked.

Mom wearily glanced up from her bills and put on her best smile. It was such a wonderful smile, Trip almost believed it.

"Yes honey. Everything's fine," said Mom tenderly. "You need to get to bed now. You have school tomorrow."

It was obvious to Trip that everything was definitely *not* fine. Trip watched silently a bit longer as Mom continued to pore over the bills.

# CHAPTER THREE

The next morning, Trip arrived at school and couldn't wait to talk to his best friend, Josh. Trip spotted him hustling over from across the schoolyard. Josh was a bit nerdy and out of shape. He was a little winded as he ran up to Trip.

"I got your text," said Josh. "So what's the deal with this trunk? What's in it? Why is it so important?"

"It's important because I..." Trip trailed off, as he stared off into the distance dreamily. Josh waved his hand in front of Trip's eyes.

"Earth to Trip," said Josh. "What's going on in there? Anybody home?"

Josh followed Trip's gaze to see what had him so mesmerized. Trip was staring at a girl he had never seen before. The world ran in slow motion as he watched the new girl walking through the schoolyard, hair dancing as she turned her head. She wore a radiant smile as she laughed and talked with her friends.

"Who is she?" asked Trip.

"Oh her, that's Sarah Valentine," said Josh dismissively. "We have Algebra together... seems nice enough."

Josh realized Trip was still staring at Sarah. His mouth hung so far open, Josh worried someone might step on Trip's chin.

"Whoa, whoa, whoa! Stop it," said Josh. "No way. Stay away from her. She's more popular than both of us combined, and she's only been here three days."

Oblivious, Trip started to walk towards Sarah. Josh reached out and grabbed him.

"Aw, come on Trip," pleaded Josh. "Girls are nothing but trouble. Seriously... you're gonna do this?"

It was too late. There was no stopping Trip now.

Trip had no idea what came over him. He was never really comfortable talking to girls, but he just could not stop himself. It was like Sarah was a magnet pulling him over. He vaguely heard Josh frantically mumbling about something, but he had no idea what he was saying. Trip walked right up to Sarah and her friends and turned on the charm.

"Excuse me ladies," said Trip confidently. "I see we have a new student here. I'm Trip." He extended his hand.

"I'm Sarah," she said as she shook his hand warmly.

Trip nearly lost his pretense of confidence when he heard her voice. It was beautiful, and almost made Trip melt. He shook it off.

"Well, Sarah," said Trip. "I am with the official welcoming committee of our fine school. I'm sorry to be three days late, but I was busy...uh...founding the official welcoming committee of our fine school."

Trip was surprised to hear the words coming from his own mouth. He was worried as he noticed a few of the girls giggling behind Sarah. Had he screwed this up?

"Well, Trip," said Sarah, bemused. "It's better late than never I guess. What does your official welcoming committee of our fine school do?"

"I haven't quite figured that part out yet," said Trip truthfully. "But I do know we will be quite good at whatever we decide to do"

Sarah gave a little chuckle. Trip was surprised at how well this was going. Most of the time, the girls Trip liked did not want a thing to do with him. Sarah seemed as if she actually enjoyed the conversation. He realized he had been awkwardly staring at her in silence as he thought. He needed to come up with something quick.

"So Sarah, how do you like... Florida so far?" Trip asked clumsily.

"I love Florida," replied Sarah. "I lived in West Palm Beach my whole life. People are kind of *fake* down there, though."

Trip stiffened his arms and body, and did his best robot impersonation. Voice and all.

"Well Sar-ah," said Trip in his robot voice. "I am sure you will discover all the human units of St. Augustine to be reasonably real, not artificial."

Sarah laughed, "Well if I meet any of these human units, I'll be sure to let you know."

"Well as the official representative of the welcoming committee," said Trip in his normal, confident voice, "I feel it is my duty to walk you to class. And on the way..."

Trip was cut off mid-sentence by the meanest, ugliest, bully in the whole school. Eli Kramdon was twice as big as the rest of the kids in their grade, and he toted four goons along with him; each one of them a bit smaller, but no less evil, than Eli.

"Hey Twit! Your name is Twit, isn't it?" barked Eli.

"Not right now Eli," begged Trip.

"Oh, is it a bad time for you, Twit?" taunted Eli. "Are you trying to get a little kiss from your girlfriend here? I warned you about how dangerous this school is getting. I can't believe you even dare show up since you haven't paid for my professional security services"

"Eli, I told you," said Trip. "I'm not giving you any money. I don't even have any money. You're going to have to…"

"You'll give me my money," interrupted Eli. "And you'll stay away from the new girl. She's mine!" He said this loudly and declared it for the whole school to hear.

"Excuse me?" said Sarah, her words slicing through the air like a sharp knife.

"You heard me," said Eli. "This is my school and I get what I want. And you are now my girlfriend."

Trip looked at Sarah and saw that she was calm and collected.

"As if I would ever date someone who would wear that shirt with those pants!" said Sarah. "My mom taught me fashion sense."

Her friends laughed and high fived one another. Sarah reached in her backpack and pulled out a can of mace.

"And my dad taught me self defense," said Sarah. "So stay away from me, or you'll get a face full of pepper."

The crowd let out a collective approval of Sarah's tactics. Eli had no choice but to turn his rage back to Trip.

"Turn over that security payment right now Twit," raged Eli. "Or I can't be responsible for what might happen to you and your little boyfriend Josh over there. Not to mention Miss Fashion Queen here."

Eli's goons started to move in on Trip and Josh. They had seen this before, and they knew there was only one course of action to prevent bruised eyes or bloodied noses. They took off running, straight through the crowd. Eli's goons tore off after them, but the crowd closed in on them as they passed through, which gave Trip and Josh a head start.

Trip and Josh made a beeline to an alley that led to the back of the school. Josh started to dig through his backpack.

"What are you doing, Josh?" asked Trip, dumbfounded. "There's no time for that right now! Put it away!"

They rounded the corner of the alley, hoping they managed to lose the goons. Josh was completely winded and looked as if he could not go any further. They stopped and took a moment to figure out what to do, but the goons saw them. Josh found what he was looking for in his backpack. He pulled out a bag of marbles.

"Over here!" yelled one of the goons to the others. "They went down that alley."

Two of the goons rounded the corner into the alley, only to find themselves slipping and sliding on a sea of marbles scattered across the ground. They grabbed for each other, but only found handfuls of air. It was quite the site as they flailed around. Finally, the goons went down hard, landing with a thud on the concrete alley, momentarily stunned. Josh came out of hiding and started to gather his marbles.

"Are you kidding me?" said Trip. "Let's get out of here!"

"Oh yeah, I guess you're right," said Josh, a bit chagrined about leaving his marbles behind.

Trip and Josh dashed down the alley. Something worried Trip, and he didn't have a chance to figure it out before it stared him directly in the face.

Only two goons fell victim to the marble trap. There were two more out there, and they rounded the corner at the other end of the alley. They were headed straight for them, and fast!

Trip turned to go back the other way, only to see the first two goons rising to their feet. And they looked furious. Trip and Josh were trapped.

Trip thought fast. It was one thing for him to take a beating, but he couldn't allow Josh to get beat up just because he was Trip's best friend. There had to be a way out of this. The goons slowed, almost to a stop. They knew they had won this battle and they wanted to enjoy the moment. Trip and Josh made sure to keep an equal distance, and an eye on both ends of the alley.

"Bad idea, Trip," taunted one of the goons. "You're only making things worse. I could have taken mercy on you before you pulled that stunt with the marbles, but now you have to pay. Just surrender, and maybe it won't be quite as bad. Don't get me wrong. It will still be bad, but maybe not quite as bad."

Josh whispered in a panic, "Come on Trip! This is not good! You gotta think of something fast!"

"I'm going to get past those two," whispered Trip. "They should take off after me. You follow right behind them and make your way into the school. You'll be safe there."

"You'll never get past those guys," said Josh. "They're huge! And did you see that one guy? He was all sweaty and probably doesn't wash his hands after he goes to the bathroom. Do you know how many germs…"

"I'll get past them," Trip interrupted. "You just make sure you run as fast as you can, and make it to the school. Got it?"

Josh gave Trip a nod. Trip was off, running fast in the direction they came from, straight for the goons that were victims of the marble trap. Josh couldn't see how this was going to work, and he was sure it was the end.

The goons prepared for Trip's approach and assumed a crouched position. Just as Trip reached them, he jumped on a garbage can, then up and across a dumpster, and hopped down on the other side of the goons. He bolted down the alley.

Just as predicted, the goons took off after him. Josh found it hard to believe. Trip's plan had worked. Then he remembered that he still had to escape. He took off. He grabbed the trashcan Trip had jumped on and threw it back towards the other two goons.

Trip rounded the corner, moving fast. He slowed down long enough to glance back and check on Josh. The two goons that chased Trip were just coming around the corner, followed by Josh. He allowed himself a smile when he saw his plan was working, and turned back around and poured on the speed. A foot reached out and tripped him. He went down hard. And there stood Eli towering above him.

"That was a bad idea, Twit," said Eli. "Probably the worst idea you've ever had. And now it's time to pay for your bad idea."

Trip looked towards the school just in time to see Josh had made it safely through the doors. The goons gave up pursuit, completely out of breath, but satisfied with the knowledge Eli had captured Trip.


Eli's goons now gripped Trip tightly in front of a gathering of students. Eli took this opportunity to address the crowd.

"Now look what happens to kids when they don't have the good sense to use Eli's Professional Security Services. Let this be an example to you all. Without protection, this school can be a dangerous place," said Eli, as he delivered a hard punch to Trip's stomach. Trip let out a groan. "My associates here will be happy to tell you about our discount packages."

Another punch flew, this time even harder, to Trip's face. Trip heard a loud crunch as blood trickled out of his nose. Sarah winced as she watched. She couldn't help but wonder if she was part of the reason Trip was getting such a beating. Maybe she should not have humiliated Eli the way she did.

Just then the school bell rang. The goons threw Trip to the ground and he dropped like a sack of potatoes.

"Now get to class, everyone," said Eli with genuine pleasure. "You don't want to be late on a fine day like this."

Eli could not have imagined this going any better. Trip played his part perfectly. This would be great for business. Sometimes these things just worked out. He strolled away to class, but made sure to stroll by Sarah before he left.

"He's not so special now, is he?" Eli remarked, and he left Trip laying on the ground, beat up, with Sarah standing over him.

## CHAPTER FOUR

By the time Trip made it to lunch that day, he had all but forgotten the incident with Eli. He and Josh exchanged theories about Pappy's trunk, which was way more interesting than anything that could ever have happened with Eli.

"I bet it's full of stock certificates," said Josh excitedly. "Or maybe some really valuable baseball cards... oh, or maybe some first edition comic books or something. Something really expensive, I'm sure. I guess you're just gonna have to wait to find out. Sounds like your mom isn't letting you anywhere near that trunk."

"There's no way I'm waiting," challenged Trip. "I have to know what it is."

"Well, allrighty then," said Josh. "No waiting for you. But on to more pressing matters. Are you going to eat that little cake roll thingy? 'Cause I really love those things." Josh did not wait for an answer. He plucked the cake roll right out of Trip's hand.

Just as Josh was about to eat his newly found treasure, it was snatched from his hand. It was Eli, and he crammed the entire cake into his mouth.

"Hey! That's mine!" Josh cried in outrage.

Trip was about to remind Josh it was only his for about two seconds, but Eli stepped in.

"You know, boys," mused Eli. "That was quite a stunt you pulled this morning. It's amazing how good it was for business though. I just hope you realize what a bad idea it was messing with me."

"Look, Eli," Trip started.

"Don't interrupt me. My mom says it's very rude," said Eli, loudly, so the entire lunchroom could hear. "Now, because I'm such a generous humanitarian, you're getting a second chance. Get me my money first thing in the morning, and the beatings will end. If you don't have my money..."

Eli grabbed Trip's chocolate milk and slowly poured it down the front of Trip's shirt.

"I guess we'll just have a repeat performance every day until you can get me my money," said Eli.

Just to drive home his point, Eli tossed the empty milk carton in Trip's face as he walked away. Trip was devastated. Everyone in the cafeteria had witnessed this scene, and Trip had just sat there and let Eli do it. And worse, Sarah saw the whole thing. He just wanted to crawl up in a ball under the table and wait until everyone was gone. But if he did that, Eli would have a total victory. If Trip was going to salvage this, he needed to do something now. All eyes were still on him, so he cleared his throat and spoke loudly.

"Well, that was uncalled for. Anyone know a good dry cleaner?" said Trip with a laugh.

Josh joined in with a laugh, but they were the only two. It was not what Trip hoped for, but everyone started going back to their own business.

He looked over towards Sarah's table, and she had resumed talking with her friends. She snuck a look back his way one last time and gave him a little smile. Trip knew he must have looked pretty silly with chocolate milk all down his shirt, but he tried his best to return the smile and hang on to a bit of his dignity.

"What's that goofy smile all about? You look like a total dork," said Josh. And with that, lunch was over.

Trip disposed of his lunch tray and made his best effort to clean the milk off his shirt, but it wasn't working too well.

"That's a nice shirt. I hope it cleans up OK," said Sarah as she headed towards the tray window.

Trip was caught off guard, and felt a bit silly about the whole situation. But then again, Sarah did say she liked his shirt.

"Oh thanks, I think the milk adds a little something extra. I may just keep it this way," said Trip in an attempt to bring some humor to the situation.

It worked. Sarah gave a little chuckle, and her laughter sounded like music to Trip. There was something about her that just made Trip feel comfortable. Only a minute ago, he felt like he never wanted to see anyone again, and now he felt like everything would be fine, even if Eli decided to follow the chocolate milk stunt with a side of nachos.

"You know," said Sarah. "You promised to walk me to class this morning. And then you stood me up."

"I'm sorry. I was a bit... occupied this morning," said Trip sheepishly.

"Well you can make it up to me after school. Why don't you meet me out front, and you can walk me home?" suggested Sarah.

Trip could not have been happier. He thought he had completely blown any chance of getting to know Sarah, and here she was asking him to walk her home. Even all the horrible humiliation with Eli would not be able to ruin this day.

Just then the principal's voice boomed across the loudspeaker in the lunchroom. "Attention, please! Would Francis Montgomery the Fourth please report to the principal's office right away. Francis Montgomery the Fourth to the principal's office." The voice rang out through the entire school.

Trip's expression immediately changed. He looked horrified. He hated the name Francis. Why had the principal used his real name? He filled out the name change request card and hand delivered it to the principal himself. Every time one of the teachers called him Francis, the other kids were relentless in their teasing. And to make it worse, they added *the fourth* to the end. When he heard his whole name, together like that, *Francis Montgomery the Fourth*, it made him want to bully himself.

"What's wrong?" asked Sarah.

"Oh, nothing. I'm sorry. I just gotta go, that's all," said Trip.

And of course, here came one of Eli's goons and a few of the goon's friends.

"Oh Francis," taunted the goon. "Why can't I have a boy's name? Please someone give me a boy's name."

The friend added stuffily, "Yes Francis Montgomery the Fourth. Report hastily to the principal's office." They both laughed and patted each other on the back.

"Oh you guys are so funny," said Trip. "Ha, ha. I've never heard anyone make fun of my name before."

He hurried away, careful not to make eye contact with anyone as he went.

Trip arrived at the principal's office to find Mom there waiting, barely holding herself together. Tears ran down her face, and this stopped Trip in his tracks.

"Pappy had a heart attack," Mom managed to squeak out. "He's in a coma. They don't know if he's going to make it."

"But I just saw him… He… Pappy said…" tried Trip.

The words would not come out. All of a sudden everything that happened today meant nothing. Pappy was in a coma and he may never come out of it. He may even die. Trip melted into his Mom's arms and they cried together.

## CHAPTER FIVE

Trip and Mom spent the rest of the day with Pappy, talking to doctors. When they got home, Josh was waiting on the front porch playing a video game. Josh really was a great friend, and Trip was happy to see him. For nearly a full second, Josh gave Trip sort of a half-hug.

"Dude," said Josh. "That's pretty messed up. You know, with your Pappy and all."

"Thanks Josh, but didn't you have some gaming competition today?" asked Trip.

"SOME gaming competition!" Josh said excitedly. "It's only the biggest gaming competition in the country!" Josh calmed himself, "Yes, I was supposed to, but when they told me about your Pappy... I mean I guess I've never really known anyone that died before. I did have a fish die once, but we just flushed him down the toilet."

"He's not dead, Josh. He's going to be fine," said Trip, not sure if he believed it himself.

"OK, if you say so," said Josh noncommittally. "Is your head all screwed up or anything? Like, are you gonna need some therapy or anything?"

Trip was used to his inability to have normal human interaction, so Josh's dispassionate attitude didn't bother him a bit. It was actually kind of nice to have someone talk straight about the situation with Pappy. Everyone Trip talked to today treated him like a fragile mental case, but not Josh. He came right out and said what he was thinking, and Trip felt comfortable saying what was on his mind around Josh.

"I just keep thinking about that trunk," said Trip. "It's so strange... Pappy tells me about this thing. More like he's GOT to tell me, and then goes into a coma. Don't you think the timing is a little weird?"

Trip had thought about it most of the day. He remembered what a struggle it was for Pappy to hold on to reality yesterday while he told Trip about the trunk. It must have been extremely important to him. Did Pappy somehow know that he would go into a coma, or even die? Did he feel it was his last chance to tell Trip about the trunk? If only Pappy could have told him more about what he was supposed to do.

"I guess that trunk thing was pretty important to your Pappy," said Josh.

"Not WAS important. It IS important to him. So it's important to me. I'm going to find that trunk, and Pappy will be OK. You'll see," said Trip.

The answers were in that trunk. If he could find the trunk, Pappy would be OK. He just needed to find a time when Mom was not paying attention so he could sneak into the attic and get it.

"Oh. I almost forgot," said Josh. "I saw Sarah after school today"

"Aw, man! I was supposed to walk her home today. That's twice I've stood her up," Trip groaned.

"No, that's not what I meant," said Josh. "I kind of saw her from far away. She was with Eli. He was kind of hugging her, and they were about to kiss. It was really nasty."

38

This was one of the times when Trip wished Josh did understand human interaction. This felt worse than getting punched in the stomach. He had totally misjudged Sarah. But he could not focus on that right now. He needed to find that trunk.

"Mom is on the other end of the house checking her emails and doing some business stuff," whispered Trip as he pulled down the creaky attic steps. "That usually takes about an hour before she starts to make dinner, and she's been in there about fifteen minutes. That should give us plenty of time to get in and get out."

"Are you sure that thing is even up there?" asked Josh dubiously he peered up into the attic. "You know I have asthma, right?"

"Pappy said it's in the attic," said Trip firmly as he started to climb.

"Um Trip, you may want to come back down for a second," said Josh.

"Don't be such a baby. It's just an attic," Trip replied.

He turned around and saw that Mom stood in the hallway with her arms across her chest and a look on her face that could stop a charging bull.

"What are you doing?" asked Mom in a rigid voice. "I told you that you are not to go after that trunk!"

Trip did his best to wiggle out of the situation. "We were just going up to look for that...umm."

"...old video game we used to play," finished Josh, trying to help out.

"Yeah, the one we played when we were kids," added Trip. "What was it called again, Josh?"

Mom boomed back, "DO NOT LIE TO ME! You were going after that trunk."

Josh jumped back, startled, but Trip was not scared. He was ready for a fight.

"This is what Pappy wants!" shouted Trip.

Mom returned the shout, "And the other day he wanted you to look after his pet dinosaur, Harry! Your grandfather is delusional. If he hadn't spent his whole life on that all consuming quest for God knows what then maybe he would have..."

Trip could not contain himself. "You never let me do anything!"

"That's because you're a kid! You have no idea what you're getting yourself in to."

Trip made his final stand, determined. "I am going in the attic and I'm getting that trunk."

Mom moved to block the attic stairs. "Then you'll have to go through me."

They stood in steely silence, staring each other down, neither willing to budge.

Josh finally broke the silence. "Um this is a little bit awkward for me, so I think I'm just gonna go now. So if you need anything..."

Josh put his fingers up to his ear like a phone and mouthed *call me*.

## CHAPTER SIX

Trip stared at the ceiling, listening to the silence as he lay in bed. He looked at the clock. It was 2:34 a.m. There was no way he could sleep after a day like this. First, there was Sarah, then the run ins with Eli, next Pappy was in a coma, and finally the blow up with Mom. He went to bed over five hours ago, and just lay there replaying the events of the last couple of days. It was driving him crazy, he had to find that trunk!

The house had been quiet since he heard Mom go to bed around eleven o'clock. Trip tiptoed down the hallway as lightly as he could. He paused as a floorboard shifted under his weight. With the house as quiet as it was, the tiny little creak sounded like a gunshot. When he was sure the house was still silent, he continued.

A door down the hallway swung open slowly. His heart pounded so hard in his chest that it sounded like a drum. He ducked behind a piece of furniture for cover, and nearly sent a vase crashing to the floor. He risked a peek down the hallway and saw the cat saunter through the door. He took a deep breath and let his pulse return to normal.

At the attic entry, he carefully pulled down the rusted ladder. When he finally got it down, he took one last look around and climbed into the attic.

With a click, Trip pulled the string to turn on the single naked bulb. Feebly, light tried to reach across the attic, but there seemed to be more shadows than illumination. It was spooky up here at night with all these old dusty piles.

Trip dug through the old junk. He pulled blankets off musty furniture, looked in the drawers and cabinets. Yellowing books were stacked in moldy cardboard boxes. He pulled one blanket away to reveal a mirror, which nearly scared him to death when he saw his own reflection.

He searched nearly everything, and was ready to give up for the night when his foot nudged against something. It was subtle, but the floor was definitely uneven under a faded old throw rug. He removed it, dust clouds flying through the air. Trip nearly choked, and he found it difficult to suppress a cough.

He pushed on the floor and found few loose floorboards that he easily removed. And there, in the hidden compartment under the floorboards, he saw it. A dusty old wooden trunk.

It was smaller than he imagined; only about the size of a toaster oven, but it was masterfully crafted with a circular wooden inlay. Around the edge of the circle were some mysterious symbols designed from a darker wood. Right in the middle of the trunk was a solid lock that securely guarded the trunk's secrets.

Trip looked around excitedly for something to force the lock open, but he just could not seem to find anything useful. This was a problem he could work out tomorrow. He had found the trunk.

He clicked off the light, carefully climbed back down the ladder into the hallway, and closed the attic entry. As he turned, he ran face first into Mom. Busted!

# CHAPTER SEVEN

Trip had a hard time figuring out what was going on as they sat at the kitchen table. He had lied to Mom and snuck into the attic, yet Mom did not seem angry at all. She seemed defeated, yet resigned. This just did not make sense. Trip was waiting for her to lower the hatchet.

"I shouldn't have treated you that way. It's not fair," began Mom. "You're a good kid and you're mature enough and smart enough to make your own decisions."

"Thanks Mom," Trip replied. Still not sure what was going on.

"Well, if you're going to get into that trunk, you're going to need this," said Mom quietly as she held up an ancient iron key.

Trip couldn't believe what was happening. Was Mom actually handing him the key that unlocked the trunk? And more importantly, was she giving him permission to do it?

"Is that what I think it is?" Trip asked.

"I guess so," replied Mom. "Your Pappy gave it to me when he moved into the retirement home. He said I'd know the right time to give it to you."

"And that time is now?" asked Trip, mesmerized.

"And that time is now," Mom agreed. "He said you'd need it for the quest. So have at it."

"A quest?" asked Trip, surprised. "You know more than you're telling me, don't you?"

Mom was very matter of fact. "All I know is, if you want to waste countless hours chasing down some dream, have at it. But you're not getting any help from me. This is between you and Pappy."

She handed the key to Trip. Trip reached out, a bit hesitantly and took the key.

"Thanks, Mom. For the key, and for trusting me."

"Just don't let me see your schoolwork slipping," said Mom. "Any sign of trouble and I'm locking you in your room until you're thirty. You got that?"

Trip was ecstatic, "I promise, Mom! My schoolwork comes first. You'll have no trouble at all from me."

"I'm serious, Trip," said Mom. "If your grades slip at all, this is over. I've seen this quest ruin lives, and I'm not letting it ruin yours."

With that, Mom walked out, leaving Trip alone with the trunk. Trip slowly looked at the key, and then at the trunk. Mom had called it a quest. What kind of quest could be waiting inside that trunk? Trip wondered if he would be up to the challenge. There was only one way to find out.

He gingerly fit the key into the lock and slowly turned it. It creaked, then clicked. Trip rested his hands gently on the lid of the trunk and took a deep breath. His palms were starting to sweat. As he slowly lifted the lid, the old hinges squeaked loudly for the first time in years. He peered inside.

Trip was disappointed. There wasn't really much in the trunk. Resting on top were about fifteen old photographs.

Some of them Trip recognized as family members, others as places around town. And the others did not mean a thing to him.

There were also a few old newspaper articles from the local paper. Trip skimmed the headlines searching for a common theme, but there was none. Sitting in the bottom of the trunk was a cast iron plate with small jewels in it. Trip noticed a few small pieces had broken off and been glued back in place.

Trip ran his finger over one of the glued stones and wondered if this was the piece of jewel-encrusted iron from Pappy's story on the beach. Was this the little piece that started this whole quest?

And then Trip pulled out the final, and most interesting item that was hidden away in the corner of Pappy's trunk. He held it delicately in his hands; afraid he might damage it. It was an old tattered book with the hand written title, *The Quest for Gasparilla's Treasure*.

## CHAPTER EIGHT

The following morning as Trip arrived at school, he heard the familiar voice that made his stomach churn.

Eli spoke up so everyone could hear, "Hello, Francis. I trust you have brought me my money today."

Trip had hoped he could avoid Eli today, but was not surprised that Eli found him. After yesterday's fight, it was certain Eli would make an example out of him.

When Trip looked at Eli, he imagined him hugging and kissing Sarah. The thought made it difficult to keep breakfast from coming up. He wished Josh had kept his mouth shut about Eli and Sarah. If it had been anyone else that told him, he would have thought it was a lie. But Josh always told him the truth, and he never gossiped. He just told it how it was.

"Did you hear me, Francis?" barked Eli. "I want my money. Now!"

"Oh, you're using Francis now. I think I liked Twit better."

"Do you have my money, or do you want your beating? TWIT! Your choice, not mine."

Trip stayed calm. "I guess I was wrong. I don't like Twit either. Try saying Trip. It's easy. You'll like it... Trip."

A crowd gathered, and Eli motioned for his Goons to grab Trip.

Trip spoke up for everyone to hear. "What's the matter, Eli? You scared to fight fair? Need your goons to help you, I guess. Why don't you just let me go, and we can all just get on with our day."

Eli's nostrils flared, and his face turned bright red. Trip was pretty sure it was a bad idea to get Eli worked up like this, but from now on, this game was going to be played by Trip's rules.

"No one goes anywhere, until I get my money!" commanded Eli.

"Well, you just need to give up that idea, because it's just not going to happen," Trip stated calmly.

Eli addressed the crowd. "Now everyone pay close attention to what happens if you don't keep up with your payments."

Eli took every bit of rage and hate he was feeling toward Trip and reared back. He put everything he had into a full on punch, hard, in Trip's stomach. There was a loud thud, and the sound of cracking bones. It was Eli's hand. Eli let out a blood-curdling scream of pain.

Trip pulled the cast iron plate from under his shirt, the one from the trunk, and held it up, silently thanking Pappy.

"Oh, sorry about that. I found this thing in my attic last night and I though I'd bring it to show in class," Trip said in his calmest voice. "Take a look, it's really quite interesting."

"You must have a death wish," hissed Eli. "Get him!"

Two goons grabbed Trip, and one immediately punched Trip in the stomach. Then another goon took a turn. Trip gasped for air as he went down on his knees.

"You think you're funny, Twit? This is how you amuse yourself?" snarled Eli.

Trip had never seen Eli like this. He was intense and focused. He was no longer performing for the crowd. This was personal.

"Well, you don't know the meaning of pain," continued Eli as he grabbed the cast iron plate. "You look like you enjoyed using this plate to hurt me. Well, now we're gonna see what kind of job this little plate can do on your face!"

This was bad! This was really bad. Trip could barely breathe from the blows to the stomach, and Eli's goons had a death grip on him. They knew if they let Trip out of this, Eli would kill them. Trip's mind was racing, but there was no way out. Eli was going to bash his face in with the cast iron plate. And he probably would not stop there. The beating was sure to continue.

Eli confirmed Trip's suspicion. "And the pain won't stop. You made a huge mistake here today. One you will regret for the rest of your..."

"ENOUGH!" A voice boomed across the schoolyard. "You boys stop this at once!"

It was Mr. Hanson. Trip was surprised to hear such command and authority come from his mouth. Mr. Hanson was the history teacher, and normally spoke in the most mind-numbing, monotonous voice imaginable, but now he sounded like an angry drill sergeant.

The schoolyard was silent, and no one moved a muscle. Mr. Hanson waved his ever-present yardstick at Eli, and then at Trip. The command and authority he wielded just moments ago was quickly fading. By the time he spoke again, it was in the mind-numbing way that everyone was used to.

"You students need to break this up and get back to class," he droned. "Oh, and what is this?"

He took the plate out of Eli's hand.

"I think I will be taking this into my classroom for safe keeping. Yes, extremely interesting," he mused, turning his full attention to the plate.

"But Mr. Hanson, that's mine!" Trip pleaded. "I need that!"

"You two have proven this can be used as a weapon," said Mr. Hanson. "There is no place for a weapon at our school."

Mr. Hanson waved his yardstick in their faces. The yardstick was so close to Trip's face, he worried he might lose an eye.

Mr. Hanson continued, "I'll be watching you both very closely. If I see either of you boys doing anything that even looks suspicious, you'll be in detention with me for the rest of the year. Now get to class before I…"

Mr Hanson noticed something on the plate and lost his train of thought.

"Oh, now that is interesting. What does that look like to you?" he asked Eli as he pointed to a symbol on the plate.

He looked up and remembered where he was. "What are you two still doing here? Go on. Get to class."

"You better watch your back, Francis," said Eli ominously. "This is far from over."

At lunch that day, Josh was more excited than Trip had ever seen him. Josh talked so fast, Trip started to wonder if anyone had ever pulled a jaw muscle before.

"I can't believe I missed it," Josh spewed. "What were you thinking trying to pull off a stunt like that? Was it totally amazing like everyone is saying it was? Jimmy said he could actually hear the bones in Eli's hand cracking."

"That sounds pretty nasty," said Sarah. She had walked up unnoticed by Trip or Josh. "What are you two talking about?"

Trip tried to remain cool, but he couldn't help giving Sarah the stink eye. What was she thinking coming over here after her bully of a boyfriend had tried to kill Trip?

Josh piped in. "We were talking about this morning, and how Trip..."

"Nothing," interrupted Trip. "We were talking about nothing."

"OK," said Sarah, confused. "I heard about your Pappy. That's got to be tough. How's he doing?"

She sounded so sincere and concerned. How could she act like this after what she had done?

"He's in a coma. How do you think he's doing?" said Trip, not even trying to hide is contempt for her anymore.

"Can I sit down and have lunch with you guys?" asked Sarah reluctantly.

Trip couldn't even look at her. What game was she playing? Yesterday, it seemed like she really liked Trip, and here she was being all nice and wanting to sit with him. But Trip was not going to be friends with anyone who could be friends with Eli.

"Why don't you go sit with Eli?" pouted Trip.

"With Eli? You mean the stinky bully kid that doesn't know how to dress? Why would I want to sit with him? Ewww!"

"Oh, stop the act," said Trip. "Josh saw you two together after school yesterday."

"I have no idea what you're talking about," argued Sarah.

"Come on. Stop playing games, Sarah," said Trip. "Josh saw you and Eli hugging and kissing after school yesterday."

Sarah looked completely sickened by the thought of this. She really was a good actress.

Josh chimed in very matter of factly. "No, actually I saw them about to kiss. That's what I said, I saw her all like, hugging with him and stuff, and then they were about to kiss. Oh, and I was worried that it might make me throw up. And after the lunch I had yesterday, I don't think anyone would want to see that." Josh realized he had strayed from the point. "I'm pretty sure that was basically what I said."

Sarah was truly appalled. "Me kissing Eli? Are you kidding me? I can't stand to be near that guy. I'm disgusted I even know his name."

"Whatever," said Trip. "I think you should find somewhere else to sit."

"Look" said Sarah, getting annoyed. "I don't know what's going on here, but Eli and I have never, and will never..."

"Hey sweet cakes," interrupted Eli as he draped his arm around Sarah. "It's good to see you again."

His eyes turned to ice as he turned to Trip. "And you, Francis. You can prepare all you want. You can look over your shoulder. But when I get my chance, and I will get my chance, you will regret what you did today."

Josh put his face right up next to Eli's hand. He reached out and poked it with his fork.

"What are you doing, dork brain?" asked Eli, smacking Josh across the back of his head. "You got a death wish too?"

"It's just…" started Josh. "It's just, I was wondering if your bones were OK. 'Cause I heard that when you…"

"Shut up, fat boy!" Eli interrupted. He smacked Josh again.

Eli turned his attention back to Sarah. "Now sweet cakes, why don't you come on over to my table and you can feed me grapes or something. You and I are gonna rule this school as King and slave girl."

Sarah had enough. Her eyes burned holes through Trip and Eli.

"You two deserve each other," she said. "You are both complete and total jerks."

Sarah stormed away from the table.

Eli raised his voice. "Bye, Honey. I'll see you after school for another one of those kisses you love so much."

Sarah stopped, turned around, and glared at Eli. She looked at Trip, who looked truly heartbroken. Then she stormed out of the lunchroom.

Eli rounded on Trip. "Get ready for the pain, Frances. 'Cause it's gonna be bad. And when I'm done with you, they're gonna need…"

Josh poked Eli's hand with a fork again, and then again. Eli grabbed an onlooker's tray and hit Josh over the head with it, which sent food flying everywhere.

"Now that was uncalled for," said Josh, as he rubbed his head. "That did not feel good at all."

"You're dead, Twit," Eli said. And he turned to leave.

He knocked one more tray out of someone's hands as he left.

"That's a waste of food, you know," called Josh. "There are people starving in… some place… some place that my mom always talks about. And they could really use that food."

Josh was proud of himself as he turned back to Trip. "That sure showed him. I don't think he'll be wasting any more food today."

They heard Eli yell in the distance, "Get out of my way!" Then they heard the sound of a tray smashing to the ground. Josh shrugged.

## CHAPTER NINE

Trip and Josh scattered the photos and newspaper articles across the attic floor. Trip thumbed through the handwritten Grasparilla book.

"There's a ton of notes here," said Josh. "The information in that book alone could take years to understand. And you're not really that smart, Trip, so it might take longer."

"You're right," said Trip. "It is going to take a long time. The sooner we get started, the sooner we'll know what were supposed to do."

Mom yelled from downstairs. She sounded happy, "Trip honey! There's someone here to see you."

"OK, Mom. I'll be right down," Trip yelled back. "Josh, you keep working on all of this, and I'll be back as soon as I can."

Trip hustled down the attic stairs two at a time to the front door. He was surprised to see Sarah standing with Mom. Trip was sure any chance with her was over after what had happened in the lunchroom.

He couldn't understand why he was so happy to see her. He was supposed to be done with her. She was friends with the enemy. No, it was worse than that, she was dating the enemy! And yet, Trip was happy to see her.

"Hey Sarah," he said sheepishly. "I didn't really expect to see you here."

"Yeah, well," said Sarah shyly. "I was riding my bike, and thought I would stop by and say hey."

Both Trip and Sarah were aware that Mom stood there watching them with a smile so big it covered her entire face. They stood there awkwardly in silence. Trip and Sarah just looked from each other, to the ground, and occasionally to Mom. This snapped Mom out of her happy trance and back to reality.

"Oh, I'm sorry," said Mom. "I've got some... stuff I need to do in the kitchen. So I guess I'll go do that stuff. You kids have fun." And she headed toward the kitchen.

Trip and Sarah stood there alone in the awkwardness.

After what seemed like hours, Sarah broke the silence. "I don't really know what's going on with you, but I just wanted to come by and say I was sorry for saying you were like Eli. You are so not like Eli. He is such an oaf, and you're funny, and smart. So, I'm sorry."

Trip felt the butterflies in his stomach. She just called him funny, and smart. His heart swelled, but then he thought about Sarah with Eli, and he became irritated again. Were girls always this confusing?

"Well, I still don't understand what was going on between you and Eli when Josh saw you," grouched Trip. "It just doesn't make sense."

"I don't know what Josh saw yesterday, but Eli was hitting on me," said Sarah. "He was leaning in with his stinky old breath and saying something about how powerful he was, and I told him yeah, your breath is pretty powerful. It was disgusting."

Trip guffawed. "You really said that?"

"Sure did. And if Josh had stuck around, he would have seen Mr. Stink Breath get a slap across the face. There was no hugging, and there was definitely no kissing. I can't stand that guy."

Trip tried to say something, but he had no idea what to stay. He just stood there with his mouth hanging open.

He finally stammered, "I'm sorry. You've been really..."

"Apology accepted," she quickly replied.

Trip felt awful. All the nasty things he said to her, and she accepted his apology without any explanation.

"So can you go for a bike ride or something?" she asked cheerily.

"I'm sorry, I can't right now," Trip said. "But Josh and I are working on something you might find it interesting."

Trip could see he had piqued Sarah's curiosity. He was thrilled she had come by to sort this out. And she thought he was charming. Even Eli would not be able to wipe the smile off Trip's face.


Trip and Sarah climbed the attic stairs and found Josh flipping through the pages of the Gasparilla book. Josh was mortified to see Sarah. He quickly put the book back in the trunk.

"Whatcha doing, Josh?" Sarah asked.

"I was just reading through that super secret book that no one is supposed to know about," Josh said accusingly as he began to pull Trip aside. "I'd love to say it's nice to see you, but you really shouldn't be here. I mean, I just need to see the Tripster for a quick minute."

Josh pulled Trip far enough away that Sarah could not hear them.

"What was that all about, Josh?" asked Trip. "That was a little rude, don't you think?"

"What are you doing?" exploded Josh. "You can't be bringing people around until we know exactly what we're dealing with. This may be just a bunch of junk, or it might be something really huge. We have to be really careful here."

"Are you kidding me? She's great!" said Trip.

"SHE'S A GIRL!" said Josh. "And what about that whole Eli thing? Aren't you still mad at her about that?"

"That whole thing was just a misunderstanding," confided Trip. "She explained everything."

"You don't even know her. What if she's a spy or something? Some of that research is like a hundred years old."

"Really," said Trip sarcastically. "A spy?"

Josh tried another tactic. "Those things are meant for your family only to see. What if there's some sort of curse that will doom anyone who is not a Montgomery?"

"Well you've already seen it," Trip pointed out. "Do you feel doomed or cursed? You don't really look doomed."

"You are totally missing the point," said Josh, exasperated. "We have to be careful with this stuff and there is nothing good that can come from Sarah seeing this stuff."

Sarah chimed in from across the attic. "Wow, this stuff is amazing. Do you know what you've got here?"

"Well do we?" asked Trip, glancing sideways at Josh.

Josh did his best to answer. "Yeah, well, uh... What we've got there is an amazing, uh... No, I really don't have a clue."

"What you've got here," said Sarah, "are all the clues we need to find an ancient treasure that's hidden right here in St. Augustine."

Josh and Trip shared a look. An ancient treasure! They had been poring over this stuff all afternoon, and still had no idea what it was. Sarah looked at it for about a minute and figured out it was clues leading to an ancient treasure.

"You still think nothing good can come from her seeing all this stuff?" Trip asked.

"Hey, I guess I was wrong," Josh said. "I'm a big enough man to admit it. She's smart, just like you said."

Trip and Sarah snuck a look. Trip was embarrassed as Sarah gave him a shy grin.

"That is what you said Trip, right?" Josh asked. "Something about a good feeling you had about her."

Trip quickly changed the subject. "So you think these are clues that lead to a treasure. What kind of treasure are we talking about?"

"I'm not sure," said Sarah. "But whatever it is, it must be important. It looks like your family's been searching for it for like a hundred years."

Josh piped in. "I said that earlier, you know. That part about one hundred years. Don't you remember, Trip? I said the book was like a hundred years old."

Trip's mind was racing. A treasure his family had been seeking for a hundred years. Pappy was Trip's great grandfather, then came his grandfather, his dad, and now, the search was passed on to him.

"That search is about to end," said Trip, with unshakable determination. "I'm going to find it. I'm going to find Gasparilla's Treasure."

# CHAPTER TEN

Later that evening, as the sun set behind him, Eli sat in his back yard and addressed three of his men. His hand was wrapped from the altercation with that annoying little twerp early in the day. In his other hand he held an orange, which he repeatedly tossed in the air.

"I don't care what it takes," said Eli forcefully. "I am going to get that wimpy little jerk. What he did to me is inexcusable. It's going to take some hard work on your part, but that's a sacrifice I'm willing to make."

Eli liked being the boss. It meant he avoided the dirty work like chasing victims, or running surveillance on people. He could focus on the fun, like giving annoying, cocky, know-it-alls the beatings they deserved. But he was going to take it to a whole new level for Trip Montgomery.

He was going to watch Trip's every move and find out what would hurt him most. Not the physical pain, that part would be easy enough later, but the kind of pain that cuts deep. The kind of pain you feel in your soul. When he found out what could cause Trip this kind of pain, that is when he would strike.

"I want you watching his every move," Eli commanded his men. "I want to know where he goes, what he does...

anything I can use against him. Sure, you'll be giving up your evenings and weekends, but I can deal with that. I'm a very giving person."

One of Eli's goons spoke up. "I've got a great idea. What if we…"

He instantly felt an orange whack him in the side of the head.

"If I wanted your opinion, I would ask for it," barked Eli. "Now don't just sit there rubbing your head. Get my orange!"

The next day, Trip, Josh and Sarah got together in the attic after school. Trip studied the newspaper articles. Some were about ribbon cutting ceremonies, or big events around town. They were boring, and Trip could not see a connection.

Sarah read through the Gasparilla book. It was full of notes, and she jotted down her own notes on a separate piece of paper. Josh was busying himself on his portable gamer.

"Ha! I nailed it," said Josh. "I bet you guys didn't think I was ever going to get through that level, and then boom, I killed it."

"Seriously, Josh," said Sarah. "I'm trying to concentrate here. From what I can make out, Gasparilla's real name was Jose Gaspar. He was heavily involved with the king of Spain. The king ordered his death, and Gasparilla fled and became a pirate. He swore revenge on all Spanish ships. He set up shop off the coast of Florida and plundered tons of treasure that no one has ever found."

This piqued Josh's interest, "Tons of treasure? Is that literally *tons* of treasure, or like way bigger, like *TONS* of treasure?"

Sarah completely ignored the question as she read from the book. "It says here that among his many treasures it is rumored that Gasparilla had the mystical *Arbol de la Lechuza* placed atop his walking stick. It says that unlocking the secret of the *Arbol de la Lechuza* will give the bearer unimaginable power."

As she read, they looked at the hand drawn pictures on the crumbling pages. The sketch of *Arbol de la Lechuza* was a tree that with branches that wrapped around themselves and tangled together, forming a sphere. Inside the sphere was a small owl.

"*Arbol de la Lechuza* is said to be carved from a single piece of diamond and its date and place of origin are still unknown. There is still debate as to the magical properties of *Arbol de la Lechuza*."

A sketch of Gasparilla appeared on the next page, arrogantly holding his walking stick with *Arbol de la Lechuza* as the handle.

"The Staff of Gasparilla," whispered Trip. "That's what we are looking for, guys. The Staff of Gasparilla."

"And a whole bunch of treasure," said Josh, ruining the almost magical moment.

Outside, two of Eli's goons watched Trip's house from the bushes, bored to death.

"Seriously, dude. Eli is losing it," complained the first goon, brushing a branch away from his face.

"Let's give it a chance," said the second goon. "Maybe we'll get lucky and find a way to nail this kid."

The mailman arrived and dropped the mail in the mailbox.

"Go check out that mail," said the second goon.

"You go check it out," replied the first goon. "Isn't that breaking a federal law or something? Tampering with the mail? Do you want to go to jail for this?"

"Fine. I'll check it out. You stay here and make some sort of animal noise if anyone is coming," said the second goon.

He made his way to the mailbox to see if there was anything they could use against Trip. It all looked like junk mail. Nothing important. A really bad jungle animal call squawked from the bushes. Hastily he returned the mail and hurried back.

"What's up? Did you see someone?"

"I was just practicing," said the first goon. "Did you like it?"

The second goon smacked him on the back of his head.

Up in the attic, Sarah and Trip studied a hand drawn map in the book. It showed the shipping routes from Spain to the United States. There were about thirty or forty ships marked with dates along the shipping routes. And on the west coast of Florida, another ten or fifteen spots along the coast were marked by an X.

"It looks like Gasparilla took out these ships around the year 1783," said Sarah. "These little ships must mark his battles."

"And these little X marks must represent his favorite hiding places," said Trip.

"This is so boring," said Josh, playing a video game. "Are we just going to stay cooped up in Trip's attic for the rest of our lives reading and having history lessons?"

"Are you kidding me, Josh?" said Trip excitedly. "We're talking about real pirates here. Actual pirate battles occurred at these places. And there could still be treasure buried right here in Florida."

# CHAPTER ELEVEN

In class, Trip tried to concentrate on Mr. Hanson's lecture about the first settlers of Florida. His monotonous voice put most students to sleep, and Trip was usually one of those who could not stay awake. But today he had a renewed interest in history.

He never thought he would be excited about things that happened in the past, but this whole idea of bloody pirate battles and plundered treasures right off the coast of Florida kick started Trip's interest in history.

"And we are so lucky to live here in St. Augustine, Florida," droned Mr. Hanson. "So close to America's history. As we've discussed, Ponce de Leon first visited this area in 1513, but it was Juan Menendez de Aviles who established the first settlement."

Trip wanted to learn more about Gasparilla and the pirates that operated around Florida. He raised his hand. Surely Mr. Hanson would be happy to discover one of his students took an interest in Florida history. Apparently Mr. Hanson did not even notice his raised hand, so Trip shook it violently in the air.

Mr. Hanson could not ignore him. He sighed. "Yes Mr. Montgomery. I believe you have a question."

"Yes I do," said Trip. "Do you know anything about Jose Gaspar? He was a pirate here in Florida that went by the name Gasparilla."

Mr. Hanson opened his mouth to speak, but nothing came out. He just stared at Trip. He was not used to students with questions. After an awkward moment he returned to his prepared lecture.

"Once the settlement was established, the original one hundred settlers endured many hard ships. In 1672 the Spanish built Castillo de San Marcos, which still stands here in St. Augustine today..."

Trip's newfound enthusiasm for history diminished rapidly.

At lunch that day Eli did not bother them. Josh was attached to his game. He finally unlocked a new level, and he found it impossible to put down. Sarah thumbed through some of her notes.

"OK, what I've put together so far," said Sarah, "is that your Pappy and Dad managed to figure out the location of the treasure." Her eyes sparkled.

Trip's heart pounded in his chest. He never thought it would be this easy. Pappy had found the treasure, and all Trip needed to do was go get it. This was great news.

"Where! Where is it? Let's go get it," Trip blurted out, a bit too loudly.

A few people from surrounding tables looked over to see what the excitement was about. Trip gave them a little wave, and regained his composure. He looked at Sarah expectantly.

"Well, it's not that easy," answered Sarah. "It looks like they made a map, and divided it into four pieces. They've hidden each of the pieces in different places."

Josh did not take his eyes off his game. "Why in the world would they do that?"

"I'm not sure," said Sarah. "I guess they wanted to protect the location of the treasure until they could sort out some final clues. Or maybe they found the location, but couldn't find the treasure."

Trip's mind raced. This was still great news. All they had to do was get the pieces of the map, and they would know the location of the treasure.

"We'll go get the map pieces after school," said Trip. "They're probably not too far away, right? Where are they?"

"I haven't figured that out yet," said Sarah.

The excitement drained out of Trip. "What does that mean? They've hidden the map pieces, but they didn't say where? There's no way. You must be missing something."

Sarah was offended. "This wasn't that easy to figure out you know. They've done a pretty good job of coding all this stuff. I have study hall sixth period, so I'll try to figure it out then."

"Perfect," said Trip. "By then, Josh and I will have the plate Mr. Hanson took the other day."

Josh looked up from his game, surprised. "We will?"

"Yep," said Trip. "We're going to go to his classroom. You can lure him away while I sneak in and find the plate."

Josh only looked up from his game for a second, but it was too late. *Game over.* "Aw, come on! Now look what you made me do. I've got to go all the way back to the sorcerer's castle. And do you have any idea how long that took?"

Trip grinned and his eyes twinkled. Josh was not a fan of his idea, but he had seen that look in Trip's eyes before. There was no use arguing.

"I never said I was going to sign up for a life of crime," said Josh. "Can't you think of any other way to get that plate back?"

"We need that plate, and I need your help to get it back," answered Trip.

"Fine," said Josh, still offended. "But if I go to prison or something, you're the one that's telling my Mom. And then she'll probably kill me. And then how are you going to feel? Are you going to be OK living the rest of your life knowing you killed your best friend?"

Trip gave Josh a hearty pat on the back. He really was lucky to have such a loyal best friend.

From across the lunchroom, Eli and his goons watched as Trip patted Josh on the back. It hurt Eli to see Trip that happy.

"Those guys are up to something," scowled Eli. "If you losers don't figure it out soon, there will be a price to pay. I've been very patient, but there is only so much I can take."

"But it's only been one day," protested one of the goons.

Eli roared at them. "I don't need your excuses, I need results! Now go get me my answers!"

The goons exchanged terrified looks and scattered.

A big window in Mr. Hanson's classroom faced the hallway. Trip and Josh knelt just under it, raising up just high enough to peek in. Mr. Hanson sat at his desk eating. Trip could hardly believe what he saw.

"Is that… Is he eating off our plate?" whispered Trip.

"It sure looks like it!" Josh whispered back. "Is he eating sushi? That stuff is so nasty! It's like eating bait or something. One time my mom and dad made me try it and while I was chewing, I threw up a little in my mouth. I would have totally barfed all over the place, but the mini throw up covered the taste of the sushi."

"Seriously, Josh. You have got to focus!"

"Sorry," whispered Josh. "It's just that stuff is really nasty. Have you ever tried it?"

"Focus," said Trip. "At least now we know where the plate is. Now go in there and get him to leave. You have to make sure I don't get caught while I'm in there, or I'm in detention for the rest of the year."

Josh was nervous. "But I don't know what to say. What do I do?"

Trip carefully opened the door and pushed Josh through. "You'll do great."

Josh was so flustered he did not even resist Trip. He stumbled into the classroom before he knew what hit him.

The room somehow looked different from the way Josh remembered it. During class, with all the students in there, the room did not look as barren and boring. Josh was so busy checking it out, he failed to notice Mr. Hanson staring right at him.

"This had better be extremely important," said Mr. Hanson in his usual monotonous voice. "I am right in the middle of something very important here."

As Josh got closer, the smell of the sushi hit him. It was all he could do to hold down his lunch. He covered his mouth, and suppressed the urge to vomit all over Mr. Hanson's lunch. It took a few seconds, but he finally felt better.

"Oh yes, it's extremely important," said Josh. "In fact, it's so important that you need to come with me right now!"

"Come with you where?" asked Mr. Hanson, annoyed. "Can't you see I'm in the middle of my lunch?"

Josh looked at the sushi. "Seriously. How do you eat that? It smells awful. One time, My Mom and Dad made me try it, and while I was chewing…"

"Focus," interrupted Mr. Hanson. "You come in here and ruin my lunch, saying that you need me to come with you right now. This better be good. In fact, if this isn't something important enough to make me want to leave my lunch, then you can spend some time in detention after school today. Now what is it you want me to go see?"

Josh didn't know what to say. He honestly did not have a plan when he came in here. He only needed to give Trip a couple of minutes, and Mr. Hanson would put him in detention if his reason was lame. Why did it have to be Mr. Hanson? He loved putting students in detention. Most of the students were in there because of him, and now Josh was going to join them if he could not come up with something good.

Josh had the perfect idea. If Mr. Hanson loved to bust students, then Josh could use that against him.

"There are two students in the gym," confided Josh, "and I think they were about to fight or kiss or something bad like that. In fact, they may be doing… that bad thing…right now."

Josh worried he had blown it. He had not sounded convincing, but it only took a second for his answer. Mr. Hanson stood up and headed for the door.

"Well, we can't have that now, can we?" said Mr. Hanson as he hurried out of the classroom. Josh was on his tail.

Trip watched through the window as Josh stood at Mr. Hanson's desk for what seemed like forever. Mr. Hanson looked more unhappy than usual. Maybe this was a bad idea. They could have waited till Mr. Hanson left to use the bathroom or something instead of putting his friend in jeopardy.

Then Mr. Hanson stood up and headed for the door. Trip ducked down out of sight. Mr. Hanson burst out of the door and charged down the hallway, followed quickly by Josh. Josh wore a big smile as he turned to give Trip a triumphant thumbs up. Trip slipped into the classroom.

Josh watched as the door closed behind him. Then suddenly, Mr. Hanson stopped. Josh was still looking the other way and slammed into him full speed.

"What happened? Why are you stopping?" asked Josh.

"I forgot my yardstick. I need to get my yardstick."

Mr. Hanson started back towards his classroom. Josh jumped in front of him walking backwards. This slowed Mr. Hanson down.

"Why do you need a yardstick?" asked Josh panicked. "Those students might be doing that bad thing right now. There's no time to waste."

"A yardstick is an effective object of authority. It comes in handy in these situations."

Mr. Hanson arrived at his door and reached for the handle. Josh blocked the door and refused to move.

Josh spoke loud and over his shoulder toward the classroom so Trip could hear him. "MR. HANSON. YOU DON'T HAVE TIME TO GO BACK IN THE CLASSROOM. WE NEED TO GO NOW. IF YOU GO BACK IN THE CLASSROOM RIGHT NOW, YOU JUST MIGHT BE TOO LATE."

Mr. Hanson was so focused on catching the perpetrators that he barely noticed Josh's odd behavior. "Step aside, or you will be an accessory to whatever crime is being committed."

Josh still spoke so Trip could hear. "OK, SO YOU'RE SAYING I HAVE TO GET OUT OF YOUR WAY SO YOU CAN GO BACK IN YOUR CLASSROOM? RIGHT NOW?"

"Young man. You are about to get detention with me for the next three weeks. Now step aside," commanded Mr. Hanson.

Worried that Trip mat not have heard him, Josh stepped aside.

Trip dumped the sushi off the plate into the trashcan. Suddenly, he heard Josh's voice through the door. "MR. HANSON. YOU DON'T HAVE TIME TO GO BACK IN THE CLASSROOM. WE NEED TO GO NOW. IF YOU GO BACK IN THE CLASSROOM RIGHT NOW. YOU JUST MIGHT BE TOO LATE."

Trip checked for another exit. There was another door at the far end of the room, but there was not enough time to make it. He heard Josh's voice again, "OK, SO YOU'RE SAYING I HAVE TO GET OUT OF YOUR WAY SO YOU CAN GO BACK IN YOUR CLASSROOM? RIGHT NOW?"

Josh followed Mr. Hanson into the classroom. He scanned the room for Trip, and was glad he was nowhere in sight. Mr. Hanson went to his desk and grabbed the yardstick. Trip hid in the small space under the desk, and Mr. Hanson's knees barely missed him. Trip tried to make himself a little smaller.

"Now I'm ready to confront these trouble makers. Let's go," said Mr. Hanson as he hurried out of the room. Josh followed him, looking back in the room hoping Trip was successful.

As they left him alone, Trip breathed a sigh of relief. That was close. He grabbed the plate and was so happy to have it back, he gave it a little kiss. He forgot Mr. Hanson just had lunch on it. Trip liked sushi, but he grossed out, knowing the taste was Mr. Hanson's sushi. He put it out of his mind and snuck out of the classroom.

## CHAPTER TWELVE

After school, Sarah waited impatiently for Trip and Josh in an empty classroom. During study hall, she had found something intriguing and wanted to share it with them. She checked her watch, wondering where they were. Finally they showed up.

"We got the plate back," said Trip triumphantly.

Josh was less enthusiastic. "Yeah, but I was stuck in the principal's office with Mr. Hanson for almost an hour trying to explain who I saw and what they were doing. That guy is like a dog with a bone. A really, really boring dog with a really boring bone... This adventure better pick up some speed soon."

"Well, don't worry," said Sarah pulling out the book. "It's about to pick up. Check this out."

Josh pulled out his portable video game. "I'll believe it when I see it. For now, I've got all the adventure I need right here."

"Seriously, Josh! Are you kidding me?" said Sarah. "Put that thing away. I've got some interesting information here."

Josh continued playing with his game. "I need some therapy here. He almost bored me to death. Seriously, at one point I had to check my pulse to make sure I was still alive.

Besides, I'm the video game king. Two national championships in the under thirteen division."

"OK fine. Whatever," said Sarah, rolling her eyes. "I think I've found a clue. Listen." She read from the book, *"The bearer of earth holds a quarter where coquina borders surround a base of lime, shell, and sand."*

She put the book down and wore a triumphant look on her face. Trip and Josh looked confused.

Trip finally spoke up. "I don't get it. Is that even a sentence?"

"Are you serious?" exclaimed Sarah. "Tell him, Josh."

"Me?" asked Josh. "Oh, sure. But first, could you just read that one more time. There was one part that I kind of missed."

"Guys! Come on!" said Sarah, exasperated. "This must be covered in every St. Augustine history class. It was easily in fifteen books in the library. Coquina borders surround a base of lime, shell, and sand?"

She looked at them expectantly. But their faces were blank. She continued, "Coquina is a shell stone found on Anastasia Island that was used to make walls centuries ago. Coquina borders are the walls, and…"

She hoped one of them would catch on. A smile crept across Trip's face.

"You are really smart, you know that?" said Trip. "I'm really glad we let you in on our little secret. So the borders are walls, and that part about the base of lime whatever, what's that mean?"

"The base is the floor made of lime, shell, and sand. So they used coquina walls and a floor of lime, shell, and sand to build the…"

She gave them one last chance to get it on their own. Trip and Josh stared at her with completely lost expressions.

They were obviously not going to get it. "It's the González-Alvarez house," she explained, disappointed. "The oldest house in Florida. You guys should know this stuff."

Trip picked up the book and read the clue again. "*The bearer of earth holds a quarter where coquina borders surround a base of lime, shell, and sand.* Okay, the González-Alvarez house. But what is this *bearer of earth holds a quarter* all about?"

"I think the quarter refers to the first quarter of the map, but I'm not sure what the bearer of earth is," said Sarah.

Josh packed his gaming device away. "Well, we're not going to figure this stuff out sitting here in Sarah's history class. Oldest house, here we come." Josh had a bounce in his step as he walked away.

"Well, I guess you've changed his attitude about this whole thing," said Trip. They hurried to catch up with Josh.

Trip, Sarah and Josh stood on the street a short distance from the oldest house. They expected it to be run-down, but from where they stood, it looked like any other house. It must have had a face-lift to make it look presentable for tourists. The bottom story of the house looked recently stuccoed and painted, and the top story had wooden slats and was in good shape.

Trip and Sarah studied the clue in the Gasparilla book as Josh snapped a picture of them. They glared at him.

"Josh, we could use your help here," said Sarah, annoyed.

"One day you're going to want these pictures," said Josh. "When we find this treasure, we're going to be famous, and this documentation is going to mean something."

Trip was so focused on figuring out the clue, he wasn't even listening. They knew the second part of the clue pointed them here, but *the bearer of earth holds a quarter* still confused him. He had hoped that when they got here, the clue would make sense. But now that they were, they were still no closer to an answer.

"This bearer of earth thing still doesn't make any sense," said Trip. "We've got to get inside that house."

Two of Eli's goons hid behind a clump of bushes and watched Trip, Josh, and Sarah head towards the Gonzalez-Alvarez House. One of the goons pressed his cell phone to his ear. It rang three times before Eli answered.

"This better be good," growled Eli. "I am a busy man and I can't be bothered."

"We're watching Trip and he just said something about a bear and the earth," reported the goon. "They're headed to some old house."

"I don't care about that," barked Eli on the other end of the phone. "Have you figured out what they're up to or not?"

"Not yet," said the goon. "But we're watching their every move, just like you said, boss."

Eli roared so loud the goon had to pull the phone away from his ear. "Don't just watch them! Follow them, and figure out what they're doing!" He slammed the phone down.

The goons looked at each other in silence. Then finally, "He should go get his blood pressure checked."

Trip, Josh, and Sarah joined a group of tourists on a guided tour of the house. They learned a lot about it from the tour guide. She explained, "The house was built in 1702 when the Spanish military outpost that stood on this land was burned to the ground by English troops. A small house was then built with coquina walls and a foundation made of tapia, which was a mix of lime, shell, and sand."

This information piqued Trip's interest because it confirmed what Sarah had told them about the clue. *The bearer of earth holds a quarter where coquina borders surround a base of lime, shell, and sand.* They were definitely in the right place. The tour guide continued on, as Trip was lost in thought.

As they headed around the back of the house Trip noticed Josh hanging back, looking completely bored. Trip slowed down to join him.

"Come on, Josh," said Trip. "We have to keep up so we can figure out what this bearer of earth thing means in the clue."

"I can't believe a treasure hunt can be this boring," complained Josh. "This makes me wish I was in Mr. Hanson's history class listening to him drone on about the founding of Florida or something. And that's pretty bad. Oh wait... that is what I'm listening to here. We need to get inside the *original* house. That's what the clue is talking about."

Trip realized Josh was right. The clue mentioned the walls and floor from the *original* house, not the new tourist version. Sarah joined them.

"Listen up guys," said Sarah, pointing at the tour guide.

"... and you can still see where the original house is," she said, "right over there. Unfortunately, it's off limits to the public due to some safety concerns."

Trip grabbed Sarah and Josh by the arms and pulled them behind some bushes as the tour continued without them. The only thing between them and the original house was a roped off area and a door.

"OK, now we just have to figure out how to get in," said Trip.

Josh was already on the move. "Finally, we get to have some fun."

"Seriously, Josh," said Sarah. "Get back here. You don't think they're just going to leave the door open, do you? We have to come up with a plan."

Josh arrived at the door, turned the handle, and the door opened. "See, sometimes it's better to just do stuff without thinking. I'm really good at that." They walked through the door.

## CHAPTER THIRTEEN

The walls were cracked and the floor was dusty inside the small, dark room. There were some old terra cotta pots, paintings, and a few other antiques scattered about. Sarah stood in the middle of the room with a look of amazement on her face.

"This room was built over three hundred years ago," Sarah whispered. "We're standing inside a moment in history." She was entranced.

The bright flash from Josh's camera startled Sarah. Josh laughed as he showed the picture to her. Her mouth hung open and she looked a little like a zombie.

"Josh!" Sarah exclaimed. "Delete that picture right now."

"No way," said Josh. "This is part of history now."

"But look at me," cried Sarah. "My mouth is open so wide, it looks like I'm trying to catch flies in there or something." She grabbed for the camera.

Josh pulled back. "These pictures are staying, so just back off and get used to it."

Trip was looking through the Gasparilla book while Josh and Sarah argued.

"Come on guys, stop it," said Trip. "We have to figure this clue out before someone realizes we're in here. *The bearer of earth holds a quarter where coquina borders surround a base of lime, shell, and sand.*"

"So these are the coquina walls," said Sarah. "And the floor is the base. So what is *the bearer of earth*? It could be the title of one of these paintings or something."

Josh snapped another picture. In the dimly lit room, the flash nearly blinded Trip. "Josh, you have to stop goofing around and help," said Trip. "You're going to get us busted."

"Oh, come on," said Josh. "There's nothing here, just a bunch of dirty old clay pots and a few stupid old paintings. If we don't find something…"

"What did you just say?" interrupted Trip.

"I just said *if we don't find something…* And then you didn't let me finish. You just cut me off. It was pretty rude if you ask me."

"No, you said clay pots. These pots are all made of clay," said Trip.

"Actually," said Josh, "I said dirty old clay pots, not just clay pots. Look at them, they're filthy."

Last summer, Trip's mom had made him take a pottery class and during one of the classes, they gathered their own clay. It surprised Trip that they just dug the clay right out of the earth. When he heard Josh mention the pots, it hit him.

"These pots are made of clay. And clay is…" Trip urged them to reach his conclusion.

"Muddy," said Josh. "Clay is muddy. One time I was hiking with my dad, and I slipped in something, and my dad said it was clay. I really don't like to go hiking, but sometimes my dad made me. I think he was…"

"Josh," interrupted Trip. "Clay is dug out of the earth. These pots are made from earth."

"And to bear something," said Sarah, suddenly lighting up, "means to hold it up. So the bearer of earth would be whatever is holding up the pots."

They looked at all the pots in the room, and all were resting on the floor. All but one. There was a thick wooden shelf inset into grooves in the wall. It held up a single pot with a small plaque next to it.

Sarah read the plaque. "La Olla Tierra is one of the only fully intact pieces of early Spaniard earthenware still in existence today. It has kept its place on this shelf since the original house was built in 1702, but could possibly date back as far as…"

Josh picked up the pot.

"Careful with that!" warned Trip.

Trip and Josh examined the pot, but there were no markings or symbols, and there was nothing inside the pot. Trip turned his attention to the thick shelf on the wall. He noticed there was a small gap where the shelf fit into the wall. He firmly grabbed it and the shelf easily slid out. Now they saw a small hole in the wall where the shelf usually rested. Trip handed the shelf to Josh and reached into it. He gently felt around the edges.

"Maybe there's a lever in there or something," said Josh. "Feel around for a lever that will open a secret passage or something."

"There's nothing in here," said Trip, disappointed. Then he had an idea. "Give me that shelf."

Josh handed the heavy wooden shelf to Trip. He examined it, and hidden in the back edge was a small hole. Trip put his finger in the hole and felt something.

"There's something in here!" Trip cried.

He fished around, and finally pulled out a very old, yellowed rolled up piece of paper. He carefully unrolled it and drew in his breath. It was a handwritten map! But it was torn along two edges.

"I've got it!" said Trip in complete wonder. "It's the first piece of the map." They stared at the delicate map piece in silence.

"We better get out of here," Sarah finally said quietly. "We don't want to get caught."

Trip slid the shelf back in the wall.

"I was really hoping for a secret passage," said Josh. "Wouldn't that have been amazing if a hole had opened up in one of these walls or something?" Josh gently put the pot back on its shelf and made sure it was in exactly the same place. As he removed his hands from the pot, he lost his footing and slipped, stumbling into the pot. La Olla Tierra crashed down, smashing into hundreds of pieces.

"Oops," said Josh. "Look at that. I can fix that... I think I have some glue in my backpack. Hang on a second." He started to go for his backpack.

"No time," said Trip. "We have got to get out of here. Fast!"

They slowly opened the door, trying not to make any noise. Trip peeked out and spotted the tour guide in the distance. She ran towards them to see what had happened.

"Can't go that way," said Trip. "We need to go out the other door."

They hurried to the other side of the room and slowly cracked the door open. Trip poked his head out and looked both ways. This door opened to an inside hallway. Trip didn't see anyone, so he opened the door and stepped in the hallway.

"The coast is clear," he whispered. "Let's get out of here."

They exited the room and gently closed the door so no one would hear them. Just in time. They heard the tour guide as she entered the room.

"AAAAAA!" she shouted from the other side of the door. "La Olla Tierra! It's broken!"

Trip, Sarah and Josh bolted for the exit door as fast as they could. The tour guide threw open the door and stepped in the hallway, furious when she spotted them.

"Stop right there! Security! Security!"

A stocky security guard ran around a corner from the other end of the hallway and closed in on them. Josh was tired and out of breath. He slowed down.

"Just go on without me," Josh said as he came to a stop. "I can't make it."

Trip stopped and dragged him along. "Yes, you can," encouraged Trip, breathing heavily himself. "We're almost there, come on!"

The tour guide and security guard were closing in as Trip pulled Josh toward the exit door. Trip pushed the door hard, but something was blocking it. He felt resistance as he pushed even harder against it. One last shove, and it opened just enough for them to squeeze through. He held the door as Sarah and Josh wiggled their way through. Trip was about to work his way through the door when the security guard grabbed his arm.

"Not so fast kid," barked the security guard. Lucky for Trip, the security guard was out of shape since his normal duties included sitting on a stool in the reception area greeting guests, not chasing down energetic kids. Trip pushed hard on the door one last time and yanked his arm free. He was out the door before the security guard knew what happened.

Trip looked back as he ran down the street. He saw the security guard pull the door closed. As it clicked shut, one of Eli's goons fell flat on the ground. He had been standing by the door, hoping he would see what Trip was doing inside, when Trip shoved the door open. The blow of the door knocked him out cold.

Eli was disgusted when his goon brought him the news later that day. He bit into a candy bar and took a drink from a bottle of cold water.

"Can I get some water?" the injured goon asked as he held an ice pack to his head. He had run straight back to tell Eli what happened, even though his head throbbed the whole way and he was thirsty. Eli took a huge swig from his water before he answered.

"Do you deserve water?" Eli barked. "This is so embarrassing for me. I can't believe they knocked you out. Do you know what the kids at school are going to think about me if they find out?"

"How was I supposed to know they'd come running out the door like that?" the goon pleaded.

Eli took another big gulp from his bottle, letting some spill down his face. "You are pathetic! Did you at least get to see what they were doing in there?"

The goon was afraid to answer, so he just shook his head.

"You really are useless! Now get back out there and find me something I can use!" Eli roared. Eli poured the rest of his water on the goon's head.

"There's your water, you loser."

He threw the empty bottle right in the goon's face and stormed off.

## CHAPTER FOURTEEN

In the attic, Trip and Sarah looked over their notes into the late hours of the night. The excitement of finding the first map piece wore off quickly when they realized they had no idea what to do next. They were at a stand still.

Wearily, Trip looked at a page in the Gasparilla book for the millionth time, and noticed something he had not seen before. It was a small, smudgy shape at the bottom of the page. He had no idea what it was, but he was sure this was the breakthrough they needed. Excited, he rushed to show Sarah, but after examining it, she pointed out it was only a smudge of chocolate from Trip's thumb.

That was it. That was the only excitement, and the only glimmer of a chance that they would figure out the next step. Trip was irritable. It had been so exciting as they hunted down the first piece of the map, and he had been sure things would take off after that; and now nothing.

He put down the Gasparilla book and rubbed his eyes. As they came back into focus, he found himself looking at Sarah. When he first saw her in the schoolyard a few days ago, he thought she was pretty. In fact, he thought she was the prettiest girl he had ever seen.

Then came all the distractions: the fight with Eli, Pappy's coma, and the start of the treasure hunt. But now he noticed again how beautiful she was. She was also smart, funny, and adventurous, unlike most of the girls he knew. And Trip thought she liked him. Sarah lightly brushed a few strands of hair away from her face as she jotted down a few notes. Trip could not look away.

Josh abruptly brought him back to reality. "Why are you staring at Sarah like that, Trip? Your mouth is open and I think you might be drooling."

Sarah looked up, and Trip looked away, embarrassed. She smiled a crooked smile and blushed a little. Trip looked back as she smiled in his direction, and this time Sarah looked away, embarrassed. She went back to her notes.

Josh played his game again. He was completely unaware of what was going on between Trip and Sarah, nor did he care.

"If we're going to keep spending so much time in this attic of yours," said Josh, "I'm gonna need you to rig me a Playstation 3 or Wii in here."

"Josh, we could really use your help on this," said Sarah. "We're getting nowhere."

"Well, what are you guys looking for?" asked Josh, focused on his game.

"I don't know," said Sarah, defeated. "A clue, maybe. Anything that can help lead us to the next piece of the map."

Trip stood up and took a deep breath, held it for a couple of seconds, and let it out. He was exhausted after such a long day, and he was confident they would not make any more progress tonight.

"It's getting late," yawned Trip. "We should call it a day. We'll work on this tomorrow."

"Have you guys figured out what that NRHP112979 means yet?" asked Josh, still focused on his game.

Trip and Sarah looked at each other, confused. "NPHR what?" asked Trip.

"On the back of the map there," said Josh. "It says NRHP112979. What's that mean?"

Trip grabbed the map piece and turned it over. There were a few handwritten words on the back. Sarah leaned in close to Trip to get a better look. Trip had never felt uncomfortable around Sarah since the moment they met, but for some reason he felt awkward having her so close to him. Her cheek practically touched his. It was hard to breathe. Luckily, at that moment, Sarah grabbed the map piece and walked away from him.

"*High above NRHP112979*," Sarah read from the map.

Trip regained himself. "That must be our next clue."

Josh put down his game and joined them. "OK, if that's our next clue, what does in mean?"

"We're going to need more resources," said Sarah. "Tomorrow after school, we'll go to the Flagler College Library and hopefully figure this thing out."

They packed up their things and called it a night.

That night, Trip could not sleep. For hours he sat in the attic looking at the pictures Pappy had left for him. There were only about fifteen of them, and they were of Pappy and Trip's dad in different locations around the world. Trip wistfully thought about how great it would be to hunt this treasure with Pappy. He had never really known his dad, but he and Pappy were close. He was surprised how young Pappy looked in all the pictures. And in some of the photos, Trip's dad was about the same age Trip was now.

As he went through the photos for the hundredth time, Trip noticed something he had not seen before. The photos were all taken in public places, and there were other people going on about their business in the background. That was not the unusual thing. But in every single picture, there was an old Native American man in the background. In some of the photos it was hard to find him in the blurry backgrounds, but in some of the pictures, he was right behind Pappy and Dad.

Trip picked out the picture with the best view of the old man and studied it closely. He had long grey hair and a bandana tied around his forehead. Deep wrinkles creased his entire face, but the wrinkles were most pronounced in his forehead. His lips were pursed tight together at a strange angle, sending small wrinkles out from his mouth like spider webs.

But what held Trip's attention most were the eyes. They looked right into Trip's soul and bored into him. Trip found it difficult to look away.

Trip woke up gripping the picture in his hand, and didn't remember falling asleep. He had been studying the picture, and the next thing he knew he woke up. That is all he could remember. How long was he asleep? He looked at the clock and saw it was just after three thirty. He must have only been asleep about twenty minutes.

He looked at the picture again, and the man was not there. He shuffled through the pictures and could not find the man in any of them. How could that be? Trip still felt the old man's eyes studying him. He could still see the tight lip grimace. And yet, the old man was not in any of the pictures. Had Trip been dreaming? That must be it.

He continued to look over the pictures for more than two hours, and again drifted to sleep in the attic, surrounded by his past. He dreamed about the man in the pictures.

He awoke with a start. The man seemed so real to Trip, even now, but it must have been his imagination playing tricks on him. Trip decided he should try and get some real sleep, so he put the pictures away and trudged down to bed.

## CHAPTER FIFTEEN

As Trip slept, he dreamed of the day's events. His dreams were different from reality. Alone at night, he snuck into the Gonzalez-Alvarez house. He looked around the shadowy room and spotted the pot on the shelf. He took the pot down and gently placed it down on the ground, then pulled the shelf out of the wall and grabbed the piece of the map from the hole.

The map was huge. He unrolled it, and instead of the map, it was a hand drawn picture of Pappy. He was young, just as he was in the photographs, but then suddenly he turned old and frail. The paper crumbled to dust in Trip's hands, and a breeze carried the dust away.

As Trip put the shelf back in place and picked up the pot, he was overly cautious. Something in the darkness caught his eye. A small red fox slinked through the shadows, eyes bright in the gloom.

Trip walked towards the dark corner where the fox had disappeared. He found himself face to face with the old Native American man from the photos. As they stared at each other intently, the old man's eyes searched his soul.

Trip was not afraid, in fact, a feeling of complete serenity came over him. Trip recognized wisdom in the man's weathered face, as if the knowledge of the entire world lived inside his soul. Not the knowledge of man, but the knowledge of the earth, the trees, the rivers, and the animals; the knowledge and wisdom of all things good and pure. Trip felt it all in the old man's searching eyes and he felt at peace; a quiet in his soul few people ever feel.

As his entire body relaxed, the pot slipped from his hands and crashed to the floor. Trip jolted awake.

He sat in his bed looking around, not sure if he was awake or asleep. He still felt a lingering peace from his dream, but it faded quickly. Trip would not get any more sleep that night.

# CHAPTER SIXTEEN

Trip, Josh, and Sarah walked through the entry gates of Flagler College. The center of the college was originally The Hotel Ponce de Leon and was built in 1888. Thomas Edison had a hand in making sure The Hotel Ponce de Leon became the first building in Florida to be wired with electricity. Flagler College was built around the hotel, and all the buildings matched the beautiful architecture of the original building.

Sarah stopped to marvel at the beauty of the architecture. "This place is truly amazing," she said. "The history here is… What's the word I'm looking for?"

"Boring," said Josh. "I think you're looking for the word boring. Now about that clue… That number sounds like some sort of serial number to me… or maybe a reference to a computer file or something."

"Josh, that was rude!" pouted Sarah. "Tell him, Trip."

"I think maybe it's a receipt number," said Trip. "Or maybe a book volume and page number."

Sarah was still upset about the change of subject, but decided to move on. "But the clue reads *high above NRHP112979*. High above what?"

Someone suddenly smacked Trip in the back of the head. Eli stepped in front of him clearly pleased with himself.

"Listen Twit. You better tell me what you're up to, or you're just going to make things worse for yourself."

"Trust me Eli," said Trip. "You don't want to go where we're going. Your head just might explode right on the spot."

"What's that supposed to mean?" asked Eli suspiciously.

"We're going to the library," said Trip. "Now stay clear... I don't want you to accidentally learn anything."

Eli had to agree with this logic. He had never set foot in a library, and was definitely not interested in learning anything.

"Yeah, you may be right about that," said Eli. "But just know this. I still remember you making me look like a fool the other day. And when I figure out what's going to hurt you most... I'm gonna hurt you. A lot."

Eli gave Trip an even harder smack on the head as he walked away.

"That guy has some serious problems," said Josh. "Now get together for a quick picture."

Josh pointed his camera for a self-portrait of the three of them with Flagler College in the background. He snapped the picture and checked it on the screen. It was a great picture of him alone, while Trip and Sarah walked away in the background. Josh chased after them.

Inside the library, Josh had a stack of books piled in front of him. He flipped through one called *Developing Number Concepts* as Trip thumbed through the card catalogue. Trip was not sure where Sarah had gone. She had some bright idea and disappeared about twenty minutes ago.

Trip spoke in a hushed voice. "OK, I've looked at authors, titles, and subjects with NR and HP. I've looked for any book with a reference to 112979, and nothing. I've got nothing."

"At least I've managed to find the most useless book ever written," said Josh. "This stuff is ridiculous. I don't know if I can recover from this number horror."

"This is impossible!" said Trip. "We're never gonna figure this thing out."

Sarah approached wearing a triumphant look on her face. She carried a large book titled *National Register of Historic Places*. She plopped the book down on the table and looked from Trip to Josh as her smile seemed to be getting bigger.

"She really does like the library," Josh said. "I am so not going to read that book!"

"What is this?" Trip asked.

"It's the *National Register of Historic Places*," said Sarah victoriously. She looked from Trip to Josh. Both of their faces were blank. They had no idea why she was so excited. She said it again, leaving plenty of time between each word. "National... Register... of Historic... Places." Trip looked at Josh. He looked completely clueless too. Josh gave Trip a shrug and then twirled his finger around his ear and mouthed "Cuckoo. Cuckoo."

"Seriously guys?" Sarah said. "National Register of Historic Places?" She paused for a moment. Still nothing. "N.R.H.P. You know, the letters in the clue."

Trip's face lit up like a Christmas tree. It was like she told him school was canceled for the rest of the year. He was again amazed by how smart Sarah was.

"How in the world did you find this?" asked Trip.

"Yeah," said Josh. "Did you tackle that one day for some light summer reading?"

"No, smarty pants," scoffed Sarah. "I just asked my friend that works in the reference section if NRHP meant anything to her... and she gave me this."

103

"You have a friend that works in the reference section?" asked Josh.

"I like the library, OK?" said Sarah, annoyed. "And it might do you some good to put that portable game thing away every now and then and open a few books. We've got work to do."

She opened the book to the table of contents as Trip and Josh gathered around. Trip could feel his heart beating faster. He knew they were about to figure out the second clue.

"There are not 112,979 pages in any book I've ever seen," said Josh. "So it can't be that."

"Maybe there's a document number or something," said Sarah.

Trip scanned the table of contents and noticed something. "These places are all in order by the date they were recognized as historic places. Eleven, twenty-nine, seventy-nine. See if anything falls under November 29, 1979."

Sarah turned the pages frantically searching, and found what she was looking for. Trip almost forgot to breathe as he watched her turn the pages. There were a few entries in the book for November 29, 1979.

"Look guys," said Sarah in a voice so quiet they could barely hear her. "There's only one entry from that date that is located in St. Augustine."

"The Grace United Methodist Church," said Trip. Trip and Sarah started for the door.

Josh watched in disappointment as they left. "Aw, man! We have to go to church now? What kind of adventure is this? Old houses, libraries, and now church." Josh hurried after them.

# CHAPTER SEVENTEEN

The Grace United Methodist Church was another piece of beautiful Spanish Renaissance architecture, a small church with three amazing archways leading into the main entrance. While standing in front, it was impossible for Trip not to notice the bell tower that rose into the sky. It was the most prominent feature of the church.

"Well, if this church is the *NRHP 112979* of the clue," said Trip, "then it's not hard to guess what the *high above* part means."

"Yep," said Josh. "Even I can figure that one out. Now get together, I'm gonna get a picture."

The three of them huddled together and Josh took another self-portrait. He checked the picture and it looked great.

"Take a look," said Josh. "See how nice it comes out when you guys aren't hurrying away?" He looked up and noticed Trip and Sarah were already on their way to the front doors of the church.

"Seriously guys," Josh hollered, as he ran after them. "This picture is some serious art."

The inside of the church was even more charming than the outside. They looked around for someone who worked there, and found the preacher. Sarah approached him nervously.

"Sir," said Sarah. "I mean, uh, Reverend?"

The preacher answered in a calm, soothing voice. "Yes young lady. How may I help you?"

Sarah searched for words. "Yes Reverend, we're doing a report at school, and I noticed your beautiful bell tower. Is there any way we could go up to see the bell?"

"I'm sorry," said the preacher apologetically. "But only the church clergy are allowed in the bell tower. I'm afraid the old tower is just a bit too fragile and dangerous."

Josh and Sarah exchanged a worried look. How were they going to get in the bell tower? A slight movement caught Josh's eye, and he was startled to see Trip sneaking through a small wooden door into a back room. The preacher noticed Josh's gaze, and turned to see where he was looking.

"Uh, Reverend," Josh blurted out, a bit too loudly.

The preacher turned back and looked at Josh expectantly. Josh was not sure what to say. "Yeah, uh, I think I need to go to confessional."

"I'm sorry, son," said the preacher in his soothing voice. "We are a Methodist church. We don't have confessional."

This distracted the preacher long enough for the door to close softly behind Trip.

Trip dug around in the back room. He wasn't sure what he was searching for until he found it. In a closet, he found a dark red robe with a hood. He put the robe on and pulled the hood up over his head, covering his face. And just in time too.

Another member of the clergy walked in. Trip ducked his head and walked away, slipping through another door.

Trip was in luck. He found himself at the bottom of a rickety spiral stairway that led up to the bell tower. He hurried up the stairs.

Trip cautiously entered the bell tower and looked around. The heavy iron bell hung from the ceiling, and the windows opened to let the bell sing to the city. There wasn't much to check here. He peered up inside the old bell but did not see anything. He examined all four walls, and didn't see anything. Looking up, he checked the gabled ceiling and the wooden beams that supported the bell, but still nothing.

Then Trip heard voices. He could not tell where they were coming from, so he listened more intently. He gingerly worked his way around the tower until he found the spot where he could hear the voices most clearly. They were echoing up through the walls of the bell tower. Trip smiled when he realized what he was hearing. It was Josh's voice, and he was having an animated conversation with the preacher.

"And you'll never believe what I did the other day," echoed Josh's voice. "I put a rubber band around the little spray handle on the kitchen sink. And when my mom turned on the water, it squirted her right in the face. She thinks my big brother did it, and I didn't say any different. Is that lying? Because that would be two bad things in one. I mean it wasn't technically lying, because Mom just assumed it was my brother and I just didn't say anything. It's not like she asked me or anything."

Trip almost laughed out loud as he listened to Josh's story. He stared intently at the wall from which Josh's voice emanated. Eventually he noticed a very small crack in the wall near the floor. He reached out. It was barely big enough to stick his finger in. He worked his finger into the crack and wiggled it around. Inside, he felt a small piece of rolled up paper. Carefully he worked it out of the crack.

"Got ya!" whispered Trip. He could hardly believe it! He held the second piece of the map in his hands.

Trip hurried down the stairs and returned the robe. He checked to make sure no one was looking, and snuck back into the congregation hall. He hurried over to Sarah, who was impatiently tapping the back of a pew.

"Well," Sarah whispered excitedly. "What happened? Did you make it to the bell tower?"

Trip answered by holding up the map piece. Sarah squealed in delight, which earned them a few unapproving glances from others in the church.

"Where's Josh?" asked Trip. "I was in the bell tower, and I could hear him."

Josh walked up with the preacher, wearing a big smile on his face.

"Thank you, Reverend," said Josh. "That was wonderful. I feel like a new man. You guys should think about starting a confessional here. It really is cleansing."

The preacher was amused. "Any time, son. Now I have some other things to attend to, if you'll excuse me."

The preacher walked away, leaving Trip, Josh and Sarah alone. Looking at the smile on Josh's face, Trip could not help but laugh.

"What you laughing at, buddy?" said Josh. "I feel like a new man. Now let's go find us some treasure!" Josh walked out of the church with a new found spring in his step.

Outside, Trip and Sarah caught up with Josh and told him about the map piece.

"Well, what does it say? What do we do next?" asked Josh. "Is it another clue?"

"No way," said Trip. "I'm keeping that map piece hidden away till we get back in the attic. I'm willing to wait until we are far away from Eli."

"Well what are you waiting for?" asked Josh. "Let's get back to the attic!" Josh bounced down the street, refreshed from his confession.

Trip and Sarah looked at each other and started to laugh. Trip noticed how infectious her smile truly was, and how her hair bounced as she laughed. Embarrassed, he started to blush.

"We better catch up with Josh," mumbled Trip, and he hurried down the street after Josh.


They clambered up the attic stairs and Trip instantly pulled out the map piece and unrolled it. He did not even bother looking at the map, but instead, he turned it over and checked the back. Sure enough, there was a hand written clue on the back.

Trip read the clue aloud. "*Look to the South and don't let them in the back door. Fifteen nickels rest below the flag.*"

Sarah grabbed the map piece from Trip. "*Look to the South and don't let them in the back door.* Something with a back door that faces south, like a building or house or something."

"That's way too many buildings," said Trip. "It would take forever to narrow them down."

"What's this part?" asked Sarah. "The part about the fifteen nickels."

"I think I've got that part figured out," said Trip, surprised with himself. "Fifteen nickels is seventy-five cents, or three

109

quarters. It's the third quarter of the map. *Fifteen nickels rest below the flag*."

"So the third piece of the map is below a flag in a building with a back door that faces south," said Sarah.

Josh grabbed his backpack. "Well, it looks like you guys have this under control. I have an algebra test to study for."

"Whoa, hang on a second, Josh," said Trip. "*You* are going to study?"

"Mom won't let me enter the National Gaming Regionals if my grades slip any lower," said Josh. "It's tough enough since I missed the state comp... I can't miss this regional."

"They have competitions for that stuff?" asked Sarah.

Trip answered for Josh. "They have huge competitions, and Josh is probably one of the best there is."

"Probably?" retorted Josh. "Probably the best? I'm not taking this kind of abuse. Good luck with that whole south back door clue thing. I am out of here." Josh cleared out, leaving Trip and Sarah alone. Trip was painfully aware this was the first time he and Sarah had been completely alone.

They stood there and looked at each other in awkward silence for what seemed like forever. Thankfully, Sarah broke the silence.

"Trip... I'm really glad your Pappy left you this trunk," she said.

Trip swallowed hard. "Well, yeah... It is pretty cool isn't it?"

"Well, sure. But that's not what I'm talking about." Trip looked at Sarah. He had no idea what to say.

"I'm glad he left you this stuff," Sarah continued pointedly, "because I really like hanging out with you."

Trip found it difficult to look her in the eyes. "Well, sure. I guess it's been pretty cool." Trip realized his palms were sweating. Why were his palms sweating?

"Being the new girl at school isn't easy, you know," Sarah said. She was talking softly now, almost in a whisper.

"Are you kidding me?" said Trip. "You've only been at the school a few days, and you're practically the most popular girl there."

"That's great and all," said Sarah, "but most of my friends so far have no idea who I am. They just see me for who they want me to be. You know?"

Trip had no idea what she meant. "Look, Sarah. All I know is that you're probably the coolest girl I've ever met. You're smart, you're fun... You're like one of the guys. Except you're..." Trip struggled to get the words out. He couldn't believe he was about to say this. This could possibly ruin everything, but he felt like he had to say it.

"You're like one of the guys. Except you're...pretty. You're very pretty." There, he said it. The words hung in the air, and Trip wished he could somehow suck them back in. What was he thinking?

Sarah moved closer to Trip. "Oh, I'm like one of the guys, am I?"

Trip was uneasy. He looked around the room nervously. But when he made eye contact with Sarah again, he saw the genuine kindness in her eyes, and he felt suddenly calm.

"I didn't really mean you were like one of the guys, I was just trying... I just meant..." Sarah was close now. Trip's heart was about to pound out of his chest. He had never even thought of kissing a girl before, and Sarah was just inches away from him. He could feel the warmth of her face. He leaned a bit closer to her.

111

Josh scurried up the ladder into the attic, a ball of energy.

"Can you believe it?" said Josh. "I forgot my notebook. I don't have time for this. I mean really…" Josh stopped mid sentence as he noticed Trip and Sarah awkwardly stepping away from one another. Trip's foot caught a box and he spilled over, falling to the floor.

"What's going on in here?" asked Josh. "Does this have something to do with that clue?"

They all looked at each other, and no one said a word.

# CHAPTER EIGHTEEN

Trip sat in history class, unable to pay attention to anything Mr. Hanson droned on about. If he was not thinking about what happened with Sarah, he was thinking about the hunt for Gasparilla's treasure. The clues mentioned quarters of the map, and they had found two pieces. That meant they possessed half the map, and a clue to find the third piece.

It was finally the end of class, so Trip decided he better try to pay attention to Mr. Hanson.

"On your way out," said Mr. Hanson as the bell rang, "I want you to turn in your reports on Spain's colonization of the New World. You've had all week to work on this, so I'm expecting them to be very thorough."

Students filed to the front of the classroom to turn in their papers. Trip sat stunned in his desk, unable to move. He had not even started the massive report. When his mom allowed him to take on the quest to find Gasparilla's treasure, Trip had promised her he would keep up with his schoolwork. This would not go over well with her.

"This will be a major part of your grade," Mr. Hanson continued. "So I hope you took it seriously. I am going to be reading these extremely closely."

Most of the students cleared out. It was time to use his Trip Montgomery charm to buy some time with Mr. Hanson. Slowly Trip stood up and ambled to the front of the classroom.

"So, Mr. Hanson. Hi. How are you?" said Trip, as casually as he could. Mr. Hanson just stared at Trip, no expression on his face.

"You see," continued Trip, "I just need another night to finish my report. Well, it's actually finished, but I want to really go over it one last time to tweak it." Mr. Hanson still sat expressionless.

"I know this report is very important to you," said Trip, "and I really want to show you how much I've learned in your class. I want you to be proud of me, Mr. Hanson."

Trip thought this just might work. If Mr. Hanson would let him have one more night, he would in reality have the whole weekend to work on the report. It wouldn't be the best report he had ever written, but surely he could pull off a B, or a high C at worst.

Mr. Hanson still sat expressionless, but he finally spoke in the same monotonous drone that he always used, as he handed Trip a piece of paper. "Well, Mr. Montgomery. Bring this slip signed by your parent or legal guardian, along with your *tweaked* report Monday, and I'll only take off ten points. Otherwise, it's a zero."

This would not work. If Trip planned to get away with this, his mother could not know that he had not done the report.

"You see, Mr. Hanson," pleaded Trip. "The thing is, if I don't get…"

"ENOUGH!" bellowed Mr. Hanson. "The thing is, Mr. Montgomery, if you don't get that piece of paper signed by

114

your mother, and put both it and an amazing report on Spain's colonization of the New World on my desk by the start of school Monday, you will get a zero. Good day, Mr. Montgomery."

Mr. Hanson turned on his heel and walked out of the classroom. Trip stared dumbfounded at the homework slip. His heart sank to the bottom of his stomach.

As he headed home, Trip tried to think of a way to wiggle out of showing Mom the homework slip, but there was no way around it. He reluctantly handed it to her when he came through the door, and she was furious.

"We had a deal, Trip," said Mom, barely containing her anger. "You could go on this quest, or whatever it is, as long as you didn't let your schoolwork slip."

"But my schoolwork isn't slipping," retorted Trip. "This is just one report, and I can still turn it in Monday. I've got all weekend to work on it."

"I thought you were mature enough to handle this. But I guess I was wrong."

"Come on Mom. I can do this."

"Well obviously you can't. You are done with that trunk. I don't even want you thinking about it."

Trip couldn't believe it. "But Mom, we're getting so close. I just need a few more days."

When Mom heard these words, tension lined her face. Her voice was hushed now, but still filled with steely anger. Trip had never seen her like this before.

"You know how many times I heard your father and Pappy say those exact same words? Too many. First it's a few more days, then just a few more. And the next thing you know, you've wasted your entire life."

"I'm not going to waste my life," said Trip sincerely, "and I will get my work done, I swear. Please, Mom."

"You'll get it done, all right," said Mom, her voice rising, "because you're not leaving this house. You're grounded!"

Mom stormed out of the room, leaving Trip in stunned silence.

Trip worked on his report late into Friday night. He made some decent progress, and he found that the quest for Gasparilla's treasure actually seemed to make history a bit more interesting.

He found himself picturing the actual battles, people, and buildings as he read about them. He dozed off a few times in the middle of writing the report, and his dreams were of bloody wars and fierce battles that took place right here in St. Augustine. He woke up and wrote some more. At five o'clock on Saturday morning, he finally finished his report. He was determined to show Mom that he could handle the responsibility.

As Saturday wore on, Mom dragged Trip to *The Good Old Times Retirement Home* to visit Pappy. It was the first time Trip had visited since Pappy went into the coma. Trip did not want to be here. He loved Pappy, and loved to come visit, but this whole situation scared Trip.

They arrived in the lobby, and Trip felt very uneasy. "I have to go by the office and take care of a few things," said Mom. "I'll meet you in Pappy's room."

"I don't know if I can see him like this, Mom," said Trip shakily. "Can't we just go home? I want to look over that report for Mr. Hanson one more time."

Trip really did want to look over the report one more time, because he had been so tired he could not even remember writing some of it. But more importantly, he thought it was a good excuse to get out of this place. Mom seemed genuinely proud of Trip when he showed her the finished report earlier, but she said he was still grounded.

"Pappy's going to be fine, Trip," Mom said reassuringly. "It will do him good to hear your voice. I'll be up in a second."

Mom walked away and left Trip in the lobby alone. He looked around at the familiar furniture and generic paintings on the walls. For the last four years he had come here nearly every day, but now things looked different somehow. He took a deep breath and walked towards Pappy's room.

Trip entered Pappy's room, not sure what he expected to see. He paused in the doorway and saw Pappy, frail, lying in his bed. It looked like he was sleeping. Trip was not sure how he felt seeing Pappy there like that, but before he had time to reflect, he noticed a stranger sitting in the chair next to Pappy's bed. The man held a book in his hands, but he had fallen asleep with his chin on his chest.

The man appeared to be Pappy's age, and he looked exactly like the type of friendly old man chosen to play the loveable grandfather in a movie. As Trip walked closer he heard the man's gentle snoring.

"Excuse me," Trip said softly. He didn't want to startle the man, but the man continued snoring undisturbed.

"Excuse me," Trip said again, this time a bit louder, but the man still did not wake up.

"Excuse me," Trip said, even louder than intended.

The man startled awake and looked extremely confused.

"What?", the man said. "What is it? Who's there? Where am I?"

The man looked around a moment, then seemed to calm down.

"I'm sorry," Trip said sheepishly. "I didn't mean to scare you."

The old man took some time to struggle out of the chair, but he managed. He approached Trip and extended his hand. Now that the man was awake, Trip noticed his warm smile, which just made him look even more like a friendly grandfather from the movies. Trip shook his hand.

"I'm Harold," the man said. "I came by to read to your Pappy since he can't be doing any reading for himself right now. Guess I was doing more sleeping than reading, though. And you must be Trip."

Trip was surprised the man knew who he was. Trip had never seen Harold before.

"Your Pappy told me all about you," explained Harold. "We were old friends from way before he was in this place. He was bragging about his great-grandson from the day you were born. I'm glad to finally get the chance to meet you."

Trip wasn't sure what to say. He just stood there in awkward silence. Harold studied Trip for a moment.

"You know," said Harold in a warm, friendly voice. "Your grandfather is a great man. Really cares about people."

Trip looked over at Pappy buried in the sheets. He and Pappy spent a lot of time together, but it was hard to recall the times before Pappy was here. Pappy moved in when Trip was eight, which was about five years ago. All Trip could think about was the fun they had playing games and talking here at the retirement home.

"We were good friends," said Harold. "He used to love going to see all the old historic sites this town has to offer, and so did I. That's how we met. After we ran into each other a few times at Fort Matanzas, we realized we had a lot in common. It takes a real history buff to go to Fort Matanzas more than once or twice. We must have visited it a hundred times."

Trip was still looking at Pappy in the bed. Something about what Harold said piqued Trip's curiosity. What was it? He would think about it later. Being here with Pappy was just too distracting.

# CHAPTER NINETEEN

After a full day spent with Mom, Trip retreated to his bedroom. He spent some time thinking about what Harold said. Pappy loved the old historic sites of St. Augustine. Why did this get Trip's attention?

This happened from time to time. Trip would hear someone say something and it would stick in his head. Generally the things were of no interest to Trip, but they would keep popping into his thoughts until he sat still, focused, and really thought about why it was important. Pappy met Harold at Fort Matanzas, and Pappy loved going to the historic sites.

Something finally clicked in Trip's mind. The title of the book Sarah found at the library had the word *historic* in the title. In fact, the entire book was full of historic sites from all over the country. His mind raced.

Pappy liked historic sites, and the church where the second map piece was hidden was in a book of historic sites… The Gonzalez-Alvarez House was a historic site as well… The first and second map pieces were both found at historic sites…that was it!

Trip picked up the phone and called Josh. He asked Josh to conference Sarah in.

"How did you set up this three way call, anyway?" asked Sarah. "Technology and I are not friends."

"Having Josh as a friend is like having your very own tech services department," said Trip.

"Gee, thanks guys," said Josh, genuinely happy for the compliment. "It's really not that hard. If you ever want to set it up yourself, all you have to do is..."

"We don't have time for that," interrupted Trip excitedly. "I ran into one of Pappy's old friends at the retirement home today, and he started talking about how much Pappy liked historic sites. He also mentioned that they liked to go to Fort Matanzas together."

"What was his name?" asked Josh.

"What?" asked Trip, confused. "Whose name?"

"Your Pappy's friend," said Josh. "What was his name?"

"Does it really matter?" said Trip.

"Well it just seems a bit rude," said Josh, "to go on about this guy that told you all this stuff about your Pappy, and then not even mention his name. I mean, he is a person, you know, not just some..."

"Harold," blurted Trip. "His name was Harold. Can I go on now?"

"OK, OK," said Josh. "No need to get all huffy about it. I just wanted to know the guy's name, and now I do. It's Harold. Continue."

Trip could not remember where he was in the story. Josh had really managed to confuse him with all the questions about Harold. Luckily, Sarah picked up without missing a beat.

"Do you think all this stuff Harold told you has something to do with the clues?" asked Sarah.

"I think so," said Trip. "We found the first two pieces of the map at historic places, and now I find out Pappy loved

122

historic places. Can one of you guys look up Fort Matanzas on your computer? My mom took mine away when she grounded me."

"I'm way ahead of you," said Josh. "Says here that Fort Matanzas was built in 1742 to guard the Matanzas Inlet. Apparently the inlet could be used as an undefended rear entrance to St. Augustine in an attack."

"Undefended rear entrance," mused Sarah. "Read the clue again."

Trip read the clue. "*Look to the South and don't let them in the back door. Fifteen nickels rest below the flag.*"

"That's it!" blurted Josh. "It's Fort Matanzas. It guards the south mouth of the Matanzas River. They call it *the back door to the city*. Let's go! Let's go to Fort Matanzas right now!"

"It's ten o'clock at night, Josh," Trip reminded him. "But tomorrow is Sunday, and we are going to that fort."

"But you're grounded!" said Sarah. "You can't leave your house!"

"Whatever it takes, I'll find a way," said Trip with determination.

Later that night, Trip's mom paid bills at the kitchen table. The table was covered with paper. She organized the bills into stacks of paid, not paid, and not able to pay. She was on the phone with *The Good Old Times Retirement Home*.

"I know it's past due," said Mom. "But you can't just throw him out, he just had a heart attack."

Trip watched and eavesdropped from the shadows. Mom paused as she listened to the person on the other end of the phone.

123

"One week!" she said. "I am a single mother. How do you expect me to get that kind of money in one week?"

Another pause. Trip was not sure, but he thought he heard Mom begin to softly cry.

"Look, the heart attack hit us hard, but we're going to figure this out and get you your money, but one week is just not reasonable."

Trip was certain his mom was crying now. He could hear it in her voice.

"No, I cannot find another place for him by then. You have to give me more time."

Trip could not listen to any more of this. He ran back up to his room, more determined than ever to find Gasparilla's treasure.


At breakfast Sunday morning, Trip told Mom he was not feeling well. He asked if he could stay home from church and she agreed. He told her he was going to lie around in bed and he would probably not feel like eating lunch. Trip knew Mom would leave him alone if she thought he was sick, so he closed the door to his room and turned on the stereo.

His room was positioned perfectly for sneaking out. They had a two-story house, and his window opened onto a small section of the roof, right next to a sturdy piece of latticework. Because Mom did not have a green thumb, the lattice was bare, which made it easy to find footholds.

Trip had never snuck out before, but he occasionally climbed the latticework to access the roof when a ball, rocket, or any other stray toy managed to get stuck up there. It was a piece of cake to sneak out the window and climb down.

When he reached the ground, he stopped for a moment. He felt guilty for sneaking out behind his mom's back.

Perhaps if he had another talk with Mom, she would see how important this was and allow him to continue his quest. Then he remembered the sinking feeling in his stomach when he heard Mom crying last night. If he did not find this treasure soon, Pappy was going to be kicked out of the retirement home, and there was no way for Mom to take care of him. With that thought, he was on his way.

# CHAPTER TWENTY

Trip, Josh, and Sarah surveyed Fort Matanzas from across the water. Trip imagined a ship sailing towards St. Augustine to mount an attack, as the men at the fort fired cannons, trying to sink the attackers. He wondered if Gasparilla's ship ever sailed through these waters.

The fort was smaller than Trip had imagined. The Florida flag flew high atop the roof.

"The clue says we'll find the third map piece under the flag," said Sarah.

"We've got to get inside and figure this out," said Trip. "I'm running out of time."

"Well, I hope you have a plan to get past those guards," said Josh. "They look a little smarter than the guard at the Gonzalez-Alvarez house. And in better shape."

There were two guards in vintage uniforms patrolling the outside of the fort.

"I'll figure something out," said Trip. "We've got to get closer."

As they approached the fort, they realized there were actually more than two guards patrolling the grounds. They did their best to blend in with the tourists as they made their way closer to a side door.

Sarah watched as a guard came through the door, and he left it slightly ajar.

"Here's our chance," whispered Sarah. "That guard didn't close the door."

They watched for just the right moment and they made their move, completely unobserved. They hurried through the door and Trip closed it quickly behind them.

They blinked as they found themselves among a small group of tourists inside the fort. Josh was beside himself when he realized they were in a public area.

"Are you kidding me!" said Josh. "We just sneaked into a public area!"

"It's snuck, Josh. Not sneaked," said Sarah.

"Are you sure?" said Josh. "Because one time when I was in fifth grade..."

"It doesn't matter," said Trip. "We have to find this map piece. Now spread out."

They started looking around. The room was arranged as it would have been back when the fort was in use. There were some bunks and desks, and an old fireplace. Trip stood in the middle of the room looking up.

"I think the flag is directly over me," said Trip. "About right here. Do you see anything over there?"

Sarah stood a few feet away, looking up. "I think we should be looking right here. But I don't see anything."

She started to scuff the dirty floor with her foot, hoping it might uncover something.

"Excuse me," Trip said to a passing guard. "What is directly below the flag on the roof? And I'm talking exactly below the flag."

"I would say you are standing directly under it," the guard said.

Trip thanked the guard, who continued on his patrol. Sarah joined Trip as they began searching for a crack or hole in the ground. Sarah was disgusted by all the dust.

"There's nothing here," said Trip. "Anyone got any ideas?"

Josh was bored. He sat down at one of the desks. "I have an idea. Let's get out of here. I had no idea this place was going to be so boring."

"Sorry, Josh," said Trip. "But we are staying here until I have that map piece in my hand."

Josh gave a huge sigh. He kicked back in the chair and picked up the picture frame that was sitting on the desk.

"What about this?" asked Josh. He showed them the picture. It was an old black and white photo of the Spanish flag that had previously flown over the fort.

"Where was that?" asked Trip. "Where exactly was that picture sitting?"

Josh showed them the place on the desk where he found the picture. Trip ran his fingers across the desktop, feeling for any hidden compartments. He got down below the desk and checked every inch of it. He scoured the floor below the desk, hoping to find a loose stone or something. He could not find anything.

"Wait a minute," said Trip. "The clue says *below* the flag, right?"

"Yeah, why?" asked Sarah.

Trip was sure he was on to something. "Below the flag. Give me that picture."

Josh handed Trip the picture frame, and Trip flipped it over to remove the back. Nestled between the back and the photograph was the third piece of the map. Trip started to laugh.

"Below the flag," Trip chuckled. "It was below the flag!"

One of Eli's goons busted in with a security guard. Trip stood there holding the picture, the pieces of the frame, and most importantly, the map piece.

"There they are," shouted the goon. "They're stealing stuff! Look!"

Trip fumbled as he tried to put down the picture frame while also trying to hide the map piece. He dropped the frame and the glass shattered.

"Stop right there, young man," said the security guard sternly.

Trip, Josh, and Sarah all looked at each other, unsure what to do. They all seemed to have the same idea at the same time. They took off running. The guard hesitated, weighing whether or not it was worth the chase over a broken picture frame. He finally ran after them, but they were already out the door.

Outside, they ran full tilt. The guard pursued, close on their heels.

"Stop! Freeze right there!" yelled the guard.

They ran across a field and through a mud puddle, sending mud flying as their feet splashed through it. The security guard was close on their tail until he reached it, where he slipped and landed right in the middle of the mud.

"That's right!" said the security guard, out of breath, "And don't let me see you back here again!" He was completely covered in mud as he watched the kids run off in the distance.

Trip climbed up the lattice, snuck back through his window, and stashed his stuff. Then he turned down the stereo and headed downstairs.

Trip found Mom in the kitchen setting the table for dinner.

"Mom, can I please go out after school tomorrow?" pleaded Trip. "I've learned my lesson. This being grounded thing is horrible."

"Look, Trip," said Mom calmly. "We had a deal. And you didn't keep up your end of the deal. So you're still grounded."

"But Mom, I..." Trip tried before Mom cut him off.

"No buts!" Mom snapped. "Now go get washed up for dinner."

Trip felt defeated. He knew he could not win. He left the room, and Mom noticed a muddy footprint on the floor where Trip had been standing. She was not sure what to make of it.

Later, in his room, Trip was in the middle of a phone conversation with Josh and Sarah.

"There's no way my Mom is letting me out of this house," Trip said. "And sneaking out again is too risky."

"We've got to figure out where that last piece of the map is," said Josh.

"All right," said Sarah. "We're coming over. We'll figure it out at your house."

"No good," said Trip. "My Mom's not letting anyone in here. We've got to find another way."

"You snuck out," said Sarah. "So why can't we just sneak in?"

"It's sneaked, not snuck," said Josh.

"What?" said Sarah.

"You said snuck again," said Josh. "It's sneaked... never mind, look Sarah's right. We'll come over and if your mom comes up, we'll just hide. Simple."

"Fine," Trip agreed. "Give me an hour for dinner, and I'll tell Mom I've got tons of homework. Then we'll get back to work."

Sarah and Josh stood outside Trip's window. It was nighttime now, and they looked at the latticework.

"We have to climb up that thing?" asked Josh in disbelief.

"Why?" asked Sarah. "Is that a problem for you?"

"Well, no," said Josh. "I was just making sure I understood the plan, that's all."

Josh was never much of a climber. In fact, Josh was not interested in anything that involved physical coordination or exercise. But Josh also did not like to lose at anything, which was why he avoided anything physical, like running, football, or climbing. As he looked at the latticework, he decided that it might as well be a three hundred foot rock face in front of him.

A distance away, in the bushes, one of Eli's goons watched Josh and Sarah. He was on the phone with Eli as Josh followed Sarah up the latticework. The goon laughed as he watched Josh struggle to climb.

"It looks like they're sneaking in, Eli," the goon said into the phone. "They're climbing up one of those things the bushes grow on."

"They're up to something," said Eli, in a slightly evil tone. "You find out what they're doing, or else."

"There's no way to listen in without them seeing me," said the goon.

"If they're sneaking in," said Eli. "Then they don't want to get caught, right?

"Yeah, I guess so," said the goon, confused. "What does that have to do with anything?"

"I don't know why I put up with you sometimes," said Eli, losing his patience. "If they don't want to get caught, then you make sure they get caught! If you're not smart enough to listen in and get me some useful information, then the least you can do is make that little twit's life miserable!"

Eli slammed the phone down, nearly breaking it.

Trip held the third map piece and scribbled down some letters on a scrap of paper. The back of the map piece had a bunch of letters arranged in circles. Each circle of letters was written inside a bigger circle of letters. It looked like a target.

"Do you have it yet?" asked Sarah impatiently. "Do you want me to try?"

"I'm almost there," said Trip, in a calm, focused voice. "I've figured out the key, and it's just a matter of writing out each character."

Sarah could hardly contain herself. "OK, OK. Are you sure you don't want me to do it? I could do it if you want me to."

"Come on, Sarah. Let the man work," said Josh. "It's amazing he's getting anything done with you on him like that."

Trip wrote down the last couple of letters. He smiled as he read the message to himself.

"Here we go again," said Trip, taunting the others.

"What? What does it say?" said Sarah.

"It's another riddle or something," said Trip. He read the clue, "*tread 219 pace 10 of iron*."

Josh grabbed the paper from Trip and studied it. "I'm glad it's you guys having to figure this stuff out, 'cause that is just messed up."

"Tread and pace are both about walking, or stepping," said Sarah, unable to contain her excitement.

Trip had a huge grin on his face. "I think I know this one."

"Are you kidding me?" asked Josh. "*tread 219 pace 10 of iron* and you suddenly know it?"

"I'm pretty sure on this one," said Trip with confidence. "I think Pappy was preparing me for this. He used to take me to the old lighthouse when I was a kid. I loved to go up so high and look around. We used to count every step on the way up. It's exactly 219 steps."

"That explains the *tread 219*," said Sarah. "It's two hundred and nineteen stairs to get to the top of the lighthouse. But what's this *pace 10 of iron* mean?"

"There are 219 steps to the observation level," said Trip. "And then ten more iron steps that lead to the lamp room. The lamp room is off limits to the public."

"It all fits," said Sarah. "I guess we have to go to the old lighthouse and find the next map piece."

A knock on Trip's bedroom door startled them all.

"Trip! Open up," came Mom's voice through the door.

They panicked, and Trip scrambled to hide the map pieces and papers. More knocks at the door. Trip was grounded, and Mom would freak if she found out Trip was still working on the quest, and she would freak even more if she knew Josh and Sarah were here. They clambered out the window as Trip tried to stall for time.

"Just a minute, Mom," said Trip in the most natural voice he could manage. "I'll be right there."

"Well hurry up, would you," came Mom's voice from the other side of the door.

"Yeah Mom, I'm just trying to finish this one last thing on my homework."

Trip looked around his room. Everything seemed in order, and Sarah and Josh should have made it to the ground by now. Trip heard a dull thud followed by a groan as Josh fell the last few feet to the ground outside. Trip opened the door and found not only Mom, but Eli's goon as well. The goon looked totally pleased with himself.

Trip gave the goon a death stare. This was crossing the line. It was one thing to pick on Trip at school, but he was standing here in Trip's house. Trip knew it was on Eli's orders, and Eli had gone to far.

"It's about time," said Mom. "Your friend here really needed to see you."

"Oh, really," said Trip, annoyed. "My *friend*... really needed to see me."

The goon gave Trip a self-satisfied look, as if to say *got ya*. Then he looked past Trip to survey the room.

"I told him you were grounded," said Mom, "But he said it was really important."

"They changed our reading assignment in English," said the Goon. "And I just wanted to make sure you got the new pages."

"Isn't that sweet?" gushed Mom. "So thoughtful of you."

The goon noticed the open window and knew that Josh and Sarah had just left.

"Oh, you should close your window," the goon said. "The air is on, and that's a terrible waste of electricity. Don't you think that's suspicious, Mrs. Montgomery?"

He hoped Trip's mom would go to the window and see Josh and Sarah on the roof, or running away.

"You know better, Trip," said Mom. "Let me close that."

Trip's mom made a move for the window, and Trip blocked her way.

"I got it, Mom," said Trip in his sweetest voice. "I'm really sorry. You're right, I should have known better. I just needed a little fresh air."

Trip closed the window and gave the goon a look that could melt ice. The goon seemed overly pleased with himself.

## CHAPTER TWENTY-ONE

Trip, Josh, and Sarah stood outside the lighthouse. It was white with a black stripe that wound its way around all the way to the top. On the top, as promised, was the observation level. And atop the observation level sat the red lamp room. Josh's gaze was fixed on the lighthouse steps.

"We have to climb all the way up that?" Josh asked, incredulous.

"You'll be fine," Trip said, but he wasn't sure if Josh would make it up. It was a long climb.

"If you keep sneaking out like this," said Sarah, "you will get busted."

"I can't be worried about that right now," said Trip. "This is way too important."

Trip and Sarah started walking towards the lighthouse. Josh held back a moment, not sure if he really wanted to do this. He finally made his decision. He snapped a quick picture of Trip and Sarah heading toward the lighthouse, and hurried off after them.

When they arrived at the observation level, Josh was completely out of breath. Trip was proud of Josh for sticking with it.

"Are you sure that wasn't two *thousand* nineteen steps?" Josh asked. Trip was barely able to understand him through the hard breathing. Josh stopped a passing tour guide.

"Do you have oxygen up here?" Josh asked, grasping her arm. "I think I need oxygen."
The guide found this amusing. She just smiled and walked away.

"OK," said Trip. "Now we just need to figure out how to get in the lamp room."

"This whole sneaking into places is becoming old hat for us," said Sarah. "Nothing to it."

She walked over to the guide Josh had just asked for oxygen. She was a friendly, motherly looking woman. Even her smile was motherly as Sarah approached.

"Excuse me," said Sarah. "But I was hoping you could help me."

"Of course," she said in a friendly voice. "What can I help you with?"

Sarah poured on the emotion. "My grandmother is in the hospital dying. She used to bring me here all the time. We had so much fun at this old lighthouse."

Sarah looked at the tour guide. Her expression changed from smiling tour guide to concerned friend. This was working.

"Oh you poor thing," said the guide, with genuine concern in her voice.

"She always wanted to go in the lamp room," said Sarah. "If I could just get a picture of me in the lamp room, it would make Nana so happy."

"Oh honey," said the worker. "I'm so sorry, the lamp room is off limits to the public."

138

Sarah put on her best cry and hugged the tour guide. "Oh, Nana. What am I going to do without you?"

The guide's heart was breaking. "I could lose my job if I let you in there. I just can't do it. I'm sorry."

"You don't need to tell me you're sorry," whimpered Sarah. "Maybe you can come to Nana's funeral and tell her you're sorry."

The guide could not take any more. She crumbled. "Listen, I'll take you up there, but only for a second. You take your picture, and then you get out, OK?"

"Oh, thank you!" cried Sarah. "Nana will be so happy."

She turned and looked at Trip and Josh. Her face changed to a huge grin. She gave them a thumbs up. She put her sad face back on and turned back around to the tour guide.

"I'll get my friend and his camera," said Sarah. "Oh, thank you so much!"

Sarah rushed back over to Trip and Josh.

"Josh, give me your camera," said Sarah.

"What?" asked Josh. "Are you kidding me? This is my baby. I can't just…"

"You either give me your camera," said Sarah. "Or you go climb more stairs to the lamp room. Which is it going to be?"

It didn't take Josh long to decide. He reluctantly handed over his camera. Sarah snatched it out of his hand.

"Trip, you're with me," said Sarah. "We'll be back in a minute."

Trip and Sarah rushed off to meet up with the tour guide.

"Ok," said Josh as he sat down on the ground. "You two go have an adventure with my camera and I'll just sit here on the ground and recover from this heart attack."

Up in the lamp room, the guide was nervous as Trip took pictures of Sarah in different places. They looked for the map piece as they moved through the room.

"Take one of me right here," said Sarah. "Nana will just love this one."

Trip snapped pictures from as many angles as he could, but he wasn't having any luck finding the map piece. The guide grew more agitated.

"Hurry up now, kids," she said. "We can not get caught in here. Let's go."

Sarah moved around and looked into the bulb. For a moment, she thought she saw something, but it was just the light reflecting off the lamp. Trip snapped some more pictures, but finally the guide reached her boiling point.

"OK, that's enough," she said. "That should make Nana happy. Let's get back down stairs. Now!"

They reluctantly left the lamp room, and as Trip took the first couple of steps down, he awkwardly pointed the camera up to snap one last picture of Sarah. He wasn't even sure if he got her in the frame.


They were feeling disappointed as they rejoined Josh on the observation level. Trip handed Josh his camera.

"We didn't find anything," said Trip. "If that map piece is in the lamp room, it's going to have to wait until we can come up with another plan."

"We'll regroup back at your house," said Sarah. "We'll figure something out, and come back tomorrow."

"We need to figure something out today. Like right now!" said Trip. "Pappy needs us to find this soon!"

Josh was scanning through the photos from the lamp room. "You take horrible pictures," he said. "You might want to take a class or something. Take a look at this one."

Josh showed them the last picture Trip had taken as he was going down the stairs.

"I mean seriously. She's barely in the frame and the focus is way back on the ceiling. What were you thinking? It's terrible!"

Trip looked closer at the picture. His mind was trying to make a connection.

"That ceiling," said Trip. "I've seen it before. But I can't remember where."

"You said Pappy used to bring you here," said Sarah. "Maybe you saw it then."

"I don't think so," said Trip. "We never went in the lamp room. It was somewhere else."

Trip made the connection in his mind. He pulled out the third map piece.

"It's here. On the third map piece," said Trip.

Sure enough, on the front of the map piece was a hand drawn picture of the lamp room ceiling.

"It's like a compass," said Trip. "And on the map piece, there's this extra line here. It's almost like it's pointing at something."

They hurried over to the spot near where Trip had taken the picture. They aligned the camera and the map piece to get as close a match to the ceiling layout as possible.

"It points northwest," said Sarah. "But there's a whole city out there, what does it mean?"

Josh zoomed in on the photo and was able to make out some words engraved in the ceiling. They were right where the arrow from the map would point if the ceiling had the arrow on it.

"Look here guys," said Josh. "It says *beyond the sentry lions*. I can't make out anything else."

They rushed over to the window to look northwest, the direction the arrow pointed. The city was huge. What did all these clues mean?

"The Lions!" Sarah hollered with excitement. "Right there!"

Trip and Josh followed her gaze to a bridge in the distance. On each side of the road, at the foot of the bridge, a statue of a lion stood proudly. The lighthouse guide heard Sarah's outburst and came over to see what was going on.

"Oh, you're looking at the lions," she said. "That bridge is called the Lions Bridge. Those lions were put there to keep watch over the city. Did Nana like the lions, too?"

"A sentry is a guard," said Sarah. "The lions are there to guard the city. The sentry lions!"

The words on the ceiling said *beyond the sentry lions*, and as they looked beyond the Lions Bridge, there was one unmistakable landmark. It was historic, so it fit the quest perfectly. It was a giant fort, much larger than Fort Matanzas. It was the Spanish fort, Castillo de San Marcos.

"Right there!" shouted Trip. "At the fort! Just past the sentry lions. That's where we need to go!"

The trio ran away, leaving the lighthouse guide alone, wondering what just happened.

## CHAPTER TWENTY-TWO

They headed toward the massive Castillo de San Marcos. Its war scarred stone walls told the story of over three hundred thirty years of rich history. The Castillo was built by the Spanish to defend their claim to the New World. It stood on the water's edge with four massive walls forming a square around a central courtyard. A dried up moat surrounded the fort, and there was no shortage of cannons here. Trip took a moment to imagine some of the battles that must have gone on right here where he stood.

As they looked at the massive fort, they realized they were stuck. The clue had pointed them here, but they had no instructions on what to do once they arrived. Trip pulled out the Gasparilla book to see if they could find any help there.

"Take a look in here," Trip said as he handed the book to Sarah. "You know this book better than anyone else."

As Sarah was about to take the book, a hand reached in and snatched the book away from them. It was Eli. He took a look at the cover.

"So, this is what you've been up to," said Eli. "You little twerps are looking for some sort of treasure."

Trip was furious. "That's mine, Eli. Give it back."

"Or what?" taunted Eli. "You're gonna cry like a baby? Or run home to momma?"

Eli did not like what he saw in Trip's eyes. His victims always had fear in their eyes. What he saw in Trip's eyes was passion and resolve.

"Not this time, Eli!" said Trip. "I'm getting that book back! Whatever it takes."

Trip pulled out the only thing he could think of to defend himself, the cast iron plate. Sarah pulled out her pepper spray, which Eli noticed right away. Sarah had threatened Eli with a face full of pepper spray before, and he did not want her to make good on her promise.

"Put that stuff away," said Eli. The fear started to show on his face. "You're not going to use that stuff. You don't have the guts."

"Bad move taking that book from me without your goons around," said Trip. "Looks like it's three on one here. And we're not letting you have that book."

Josh heard the words *three* on one and realized that he was expected to participate in this. He pulled out his camera and held it up like a weapon. He took a picture of Eli.

"And next time I use the flash," said Josh, in his most menacing voice.

"If this book leads to a treasure," said Eli, "then the only person to find it, is going to be me."

Eli took off running, the trio pursuing. Eli was fast.

He ran into the inner courtyard of the castle where a war reenactment was taking place. Cannons fired. Muskets blasted. It was chaos. A troop of soldiers marched by wearing long red ornate jackets, white pants, and authentic hats. Eli pushed some of them out of the way as he plowed through.

Trip was close behind. Eli jumped over some dead soldiers, who sat up to see what was going on. Trip weaved around them, slowing him down a bit. Josh and Sarah were falling behind.

Eli ran up a massive stone staircase leading to the second level, Trip matching his every move. Eli made his way to the inside of the fort, followed closely by Trip.

Inside, they weaved through the rooms until Eli found a spiral staircase leading back down to the ground level. Eli busted through a door that led to the outside of the fort. He jumped over a row of old cannons that were lined up like soldiers.

Trip stopped at the sight of the cannons as Eli gained distance, and eventually disappeared. Josh and Sarah finally caught up, totally winded.

"You had him," said Josh. "Why did you stop? You let him get away with the book."

"Eli may have the book," Trip said with confidence. "But I know where the last piece of the map is."

Josh and Sarah were speechless. They waited in silent anticipation for Trip's next move. Trip just sat there, not taking his eyes off the row of cannons.

"Every night when I go to bed," Trip finally continued, "I look at those pictures we found in the box. There's one of Pappy and my dad when he was a kid. Dad looks so miserable in that picture. Pappy had him in such a cheesy pose."

"And that helps us know where the map piece is because..." asked Josh.

Trip finally looked up from the cannons. He looked at Josh and Sarah. It was just dumb luck really. If Eli had not

145

stolen the book and led him to this exact spot, they may never have found the final map piece.

"Because in the cheesy pose," Trip continued, "Dad and Pappy are both kneeling on the ground, pointing in the barrel of that cannon right there."

Trip pointed to one of the cannons. They walked over to its opening and peered down the barrel. He was so sure the map piece was in there that he had not even entertained the idea that it might just be a coincidence. What if it was not in the cannon? It had to be.

Trip reached his arm in the cannon and felt around. Sure enough, he pulled out the final piece of the map. Victory!

Away from the fort, they put the four pieces of the map together for the first time. The fourth piece had a red X on it.

"Well, there it is," said Josh. "We know where the treasure is. X marks the spot... So where exactly is that X?"

"It looks like they traced the treasure to The Fountain of Youth Archaeological Park," said Sarah.

"That was so easy!" said Josh. "Let's go get the treasure."

"You're right," said Trip, puzzled. "It *was* easy, too easy. If they knew where the treasure was, why couldn't they find it?"

They all looked at each other. None of them had an answer.

## CHAPTER TWENTY-THREE

Trip, Josh, and Sarah talked over each other's words all the way to Trip's house. The excitement crackled like electricity as they discussed finding the final map piece and about how Trip had chased Eli down. They tossed ideas back and forth about why Pappy had not been able to find the treasure even though he knew where it was. They were no closer to solving the mystery by the time they got to Trip's house.

"Uh oh," said Josh, as they arrived in Trip's driveway.

Trip looked up and stopped dead in his tracks. Mom was standing there waiting for him. She was furious.

"I can't believe you!" Mom blasted. "Any of you! What were you thinking?"

Trip opened his mouth to answer, but Mom cut him off before he could even form a thought.

"Don't answer that!" said Mom. "I don't want to hear it. Any answer to that question is only going to make me angrier. This is over! I've taken everything, including that trunk, and locked it all away for good!"

Trip, Josh, and Sarah looked concerned. They were getting so close to solving this, to finding Gasparilla's treasure.

And now, if Mom had locked away all their research, it would seriously slow them down.

"I know what you're thinking," said Mom, her voice now earsplitting. "You're thinking you will still find a way to go after that treasure behind my back. But rest assured, I am going to be watching every move you make, Francis Montgomery. So you better straighten up."

Mom stared icily at Sarah and Josh. They looked as if someone had just shot them with a freeze ray. The expressions on their faces were pure horror.

"And you two," she spat. "Go home! NOW!"

Sarah and Josh turned and hightailed it down the driveway without a word.

Trip cowered on his bed as Mom towered over him. She had regained control of her volume, but she was still irate. She was finishing up an hour long lecture.

"I meant what I said, Trip," warned Mom. "I'll be watching you now. I thought I could trust you, but obviously I was wrong."

"Mom, we're getting so close." Trip pleaded, which just made Mom more irritated.

"That's what your father used to tell me," said Mom. "We're getting so close. That's why he lost his job, that's why he was always gone... Because he was always so close. I've got enough to deal with right now without having to worry about you and that treasure."

Things were really bad if Mom was dragging Dad into it. She rarely mentioned him.

"Mom, I'm sorry," Trip said, and he meant it. "I just wanted to..."

"You think you're sorry now," barked Mom. "You don't know sorry. I've taken away your cell phone, there's a lock on your window, and I haven't decided if you'll ever be able to leave your room again. You've gone too far this time, Trip. I'm disappointed in you."

With that, Mom stormed out of the room and slammed the door behind her. Trip buried his head in his hands. How could this day have taken such a drastic turn? One minute he could almost feel the treasure in his hands, and in the blink of an eye, it was a distant dream.

Late that night, Trip sat in bed looking at the map pieces. He tried to focus on the positive things after Mom's earlier tirade. She did not realize he still had the map pieces, or the cast iron plate he had tucked away in his clothes.

He rotated the map pieces and held them up to the light, hoping he might find the missing piece of the puzzle. He lined them up in different ways on his bed, looking for something they had missed. He would not sleep until he figured out why Pappy had not found the treasure.

He moved to his desk, and placed the map pieces back in their proper positions. Then he just sat at his desk studying the map for what must have been an hour. It simply made no sense. Pappy figured out exactly where the treasure was, and yet he did not find it.

Trip looked closely at the details of the map, and decided to focus on some of the strange symbols that worked their way across all four pieces of the map. They resembled markings from an ancient cave wall. The symbols formed a large circle around the entire map. Another smaller circle of symbols was directly inside the larger circle. He spent the next three hours scrutinizing the symbols.

He found himself in a world between sleep and waking as he stared at the symbols. He was so tired, he found it difficult to keep his eyes open. But he was not going to stop until he figured this out. Pappy was counting on him.

His brain started playing tricks on him. At one point he saw a picture of a red fox on the map. It was not there before, and it started to move. The fox's bright eyes caught his for a moment, and then started dashing around the map. As the fox ran, it changed into a man, a Native American man. The man's face grew larger and seemed to rise out of the map in a cloud of smoke. The smoke held its shape, and Trip realized it was the man he had dreamed about the other night. He spoke to Trip in broken English with a voice that carried the wisdom of a thousand years.

"If you are found worthy and choose path of wisdom," said the old man, "then you keep forever, the gift of understanding we give you. If you abuse this gift, or choose path of selfish ways, then you are not the person we think you are. We search thousands of years for *Guardian of Knowledge*, and we finally find you."

The smoke dissolved back into the map, gradually becoming the drawing of the man, and then finally back to a fox. The fox ran away, becoming smaller and smaller until it was the same size as one of the symbols that formed the circles on the map. The fox trotted to the center of the circles and sat down. He looked at Trip intently for a moment, and then transformed into a symbol that strongly resembled a fox. Trip stared at the symbol as it seemed to dissolve through the paper with a golden glow until it was gone.

Trip was so tired and he stared at the map in confusion. His eyelids felt like lead weights and he found it hard to keep his eyes focused. He could not resist the need for sleep any longer.

Trip woke up with his cheek lying on the desk and realized it had all been a dream. As he thought about the old man's words, it all seemed real. He said something about being *worthy*. Was this a test of Trip's character? He also said something about a *gift of understanding* and *choosing the path of wisdom*. All Trip wanted to do was make sure Pappy was safe, and to do that he had to find the treasure. Then he said something about Trip being the *Guardian of Knowledge*. This made no sense to Trip, but he was wasting time worrying about a dream, when he needed to be figuring out where the treasure was.

He reached down and touched the spot on the map where the fox symbol had been. It seemed so real, but the symbol was not there. He turned the map over and next to the hand written clues was a symbol that had not been there before. He expected it to look like a fox, but it more closely resembled an owl. He could not explain it, but his brain was making connections. He realized he had seen all the symbols before.

He pulled the cast iron plate from its hiding place, and there they were! All the symbols were on the plate, just as they appeared on the map. They were faded and worn, but they were there. The symbols were imprinted in a circle around the plate's rim, making the same circle as the map. The inner circle was there too. Trip must have noticed the symbols on the plate in the many hours he spent looking at all the stuff Pappy left him, but he never realized they were important.

He checked each symbol, looking for the owl, but he could not find it. He flipped the plate over, and Trip could have sworn he saw a faint golden glow that vanished the moment he turned the plate over. In the center of the plate was the imprint of the owl symbol. It was not faint. In fact, it looked like it had just been made. Trip remembered seeing a symbol there before, but it was not an owl. He had a feeling it may have been a fox.

Things started to make sense to Trip. He didn't know why, they just did. Maybe the old man in the smoke had really given him a *gift of understanding*. The symbols in the circles were like map locators. If you drew a line between two matching symbols, and then another line through two other matching symbols, the point where the lines crossed would mark the treasure.

Down in the lower corner of the map were some of Pappy's hand written calculations using the symbols. From what Trip could tell, the circle of symbols needed to be rotated a certain number of degrees before the lines could be drawn to find the treasure. Trip wasn't sure how Pappy came up with the proper rotation and symbol matches, but he suspected the answer would be in the Gasparilla book. Why did he let Eli run off with that book?

It did not matter. Trip could work his way backwards from Pappy's conclusions. Each symbol represented a number or a direction. He didn't really know what each symbol meant, but he got the basic idea. Trip spent the next four hours trying to figure out each symbol's meaning, and then he saw something that changed everything. There was a single symbol in Pappy's calculations that he could not find anywhere else. It was the fox symbol, and Pappy should have used the owl symbol.

"They made a mistake," he said softly. "They were looking in the wrong place."

# CHAPTER TWENTY-FOUR

Josh and Sarah sat in the lunchroom, an empty seat at their table. They were talking about Trip. Trip was supposed to have math with Josh second period, but he never showed up. Finally, nervous and tired, Trip arrived and flopped down at their table.

"Where were you?" Josh asked. "You weren't in class."

"What happened with your Mom?" asked Sarah. "Is she still mad at me? I sure hope she isn't mad at me." Her brow wrinkled anxiously.

"You know," said Josh casually, "when I didn't see you this morning, I thought about calling the police. I was pretty sure that she killed you."

"No," said Trip wearily. "Nothing like that. Look. I want you guys to see this."

Trip quickly laid out the map pieces on the table. Although tired, he was talking so fast that he sounded like an auctioneer.

"OK, check this out," Trip started. "I looked at the map, and I realized that these symbols matched the symbols on the old cast iron plate and when I compared them to the map they're exactly the same. And because I didn't have the book, I had to figure out how they used the symbols as map coordinates, and when I substituted the fox symbol with the owl symbol from the old man, there it was..." He had to stop to take a breath.

Josh and Sarah looked at Trip like he had completely lost it.

"Did you by any chance stay up all night trying to figure this out," asked Sarah, "and then drink a ton of coffee to try and stay awake?"

"Well, yeah," said Trip, eyes wide. "How did you know? Did you know I've never had coffee before? It seems to really help you stay awake."

"Dude," said Josh. "I don't know what your mom did to you, but you have completely lost it."

"Slow down, Trip," said Sarah. "You're not making sense. What's going on?"

Trip took a deep breath and gathered himself before he spoke again. He grinned like a Cheshire cat.

"All that matters is," said Trip at a normal speed, "is that they were looking in the wrong place. That's why they couldn't find the treasure. They were looking in the wrong place!"

"Are you serious?" said Josh, gripping the side of the table in disbelief.

"Yes," said Trip. "I compared the plate to the map, and figured out how Dad and Pappy read the symbols."

"But they were wrong?" asked Sarah.

"That's right," said Trip. "When I checked the map against the plate, it all matched. But there was one symbol out of place. There is an old faded symbol on the back of the plate, and when added to the original sequence, it changes the way you rotate the numbers by a small amount. They used the little fox symbol thing, but it's supposed to be the little owl looking one."

Trip decided not to mention the man that appeared in smoke. He thought that would be too much.

"Brother," said Josh. "I thought you were losing me, but it turns out I was lost before you even started."

"Look at this symbol," said Trip patiently, referring to the underside of the plate. The owl symbol was still there, but it no longer appeared new. It looked as worn and old as the rest of the symbols. "That is the owl symbol. But..." said Trip, "it should be right here." He pointed at the fox symbol on the map.

Sarah and Josh raised their eyebrows, shaking their heads. "Huh?" said Josh.

"It doesn't matter, guys," said Trip. "The point is, I know where it is. I know where to find Gasparilla's treasure."

Josh and Sarah exchanged a worried look. Earlier, they discussed how this treasure hunt was leading Trip in the wrong direction. He was forgetting his homework and sneaking out, and they realized they were partially to blame. And now he was talking complete nonsense.

Moments later, Trip finished laying out some satellite images he had printed off the internet.

"Where did you get those?" asked Josh. "I thought your mom took your computer."

"She did," said Trip. "That's why I was late today. I went to the copy center up on the corner and used their internet."

Trip referred to the satellite images as he continued.

"They were looking here, at the Fountain of Youth. But when I rearranged the grid lines according to the new shifting symbol..."

"Cut to the chase," said Josh. "I'm trying to decide whether to believe you, or have you put in the loony bin."

"OK, fine," said Trip. "When you add in the new information, we need to go right here."

Trip pointed to an area very close to the original X on the map. It was just off the designated paths, but still within the Fountain of Youth Park.

"Are you sure?" asked Sarah. "This sounds crazy!"

"Yes, I'm sure!" said Trip, determined. "We're skipping school tomorrow, and we're going to find that treasure."

After school, Trip was in a hurry to get home. He did not want Mom to have any reason to suspect he was up to something. He was alone when Eli approached.

"Look, Twit," said Eli.

"It's Trip," said Trip.

"Look, Twit," Eli repeated. You're going to tell me why you've been running all over St. Augustine. I've been looking through that book of yours and I have some questions."

Sarah and Josh caught up, and Sarah raised her mace.

"What's going on here?" Sarah asked, mace aimed right at Eli's face.

"How many times you gonna pull out that mace?" Eli asked.

"Until I need to use it," said Sarah. "After that, I probably won't have to pull it out again because you'll be blind."

"Listen, I know this book leads to some sort of treasure," said Eli.

Trip put on the worst acting job imaginable.

"I don't know what you're talking about," said Trip. "Do you guys know what he's talking about?"

"No, I don't know anything about any treasure," said Sarah, joining in, although she was not sure where Trip was going with this.

"Sure you do, guys," said Josh. "That's what we've been doing for the past couple of..."

Josh stops mid sentence as he catches on. "Oh. I mean, no. I don't know anything."

"You're going to tell me where that treasure is, or I'm going to show your face where the ground is," threatened Eli. " Every day until you do tell me."

"If you don't find it by tomorrow," said Trip, "it will be too late, because that's when we're going to get it."

"Trip!" Sarah squeaked, surprised.

"Oh, did little Twit let something slip?" asked Eli mockingly. "Watch your back, Francis! That treasure is mine."

Eli walked away, knocking all of Josh's books out of his hands with a resounding whack.

"Why did you do that, Trip?" asked Sarah. "Now he's going to try to stop us."

"I'm counting on it," said Trip calmly.

"You really are losing it, Trip," said Josh as he gathered his books. "What are you talking about?"

"Well," Trip said smugly. "I'm sure we'll need that book tomorrow. And..."

He left the words hanging there for them to complete.

"Eli has the book," said Sarah, getting it.

Trip and Sarah start walking away. Josh picked up his last book and chased after them.

"Yeah, Eli has the book," Josh said. "I was going to say that, you know."

That night, Trip was in bed looking at an old picture. Pappy and Dad were smiling on either side of Trip, and they were all much younger. It was one of the only pictures he had of his dad. His Pappy and his dad both hunted for this treasure, but he was going to be the one to find it.

There was a knock at the door. "Trip!" Mom called, and Trip told her to come in.

"Pappy's OK," said Mom through her tears. "He just came out of his coma."

"Really! Are you serious? Can we go see him?"

"He's resting," said Mom. "But we'll go see him after school tomorrow."

Mom gave Trip a huge hug, not wanting to let him go. Trip could not believe how full his heart was. First he figured out where the treasure was, and now Pappy was going to be OK. Trip could hardly wait to tell him all the things he had learned about the treasure. And if things went well tomorrow, he could tell Pappy he found it.

"Everything's getting better, Mom," said Trip. "This is just the beginning. You'll see."

Mom hugged him a little harder.

## CHAPTER TWENTY-FIVE

Trip met Josh and Sarah on the way to school. They each had backpacks full of gear they thought they might need for a proper treasure hunt.

"OK, so is everyone well rested and ready for this?" Trip asked.

"I guess so," said Josh. "Are you sure my mom isn't going to find out? Because, if my mom finds out I skipped school today, I'm a dead man. And worse, she isn't going to let me compete in the regional gaming competition."

"Stop worrying Josh," said Sarah. "You're with your two best friends here. Now get your camera out. I want a picture of this momentous occasion."

Josh took out his camera and snapped a picture of the three of them. Sarah and Trip peered over Josh's shoulder at the screen.

"Look at that," said Sarah. "We make a pretty good team, don't we?"

Trip looked at Sarah and Josh, and he thought about how much they had done for him over the past week. There were fights with Eli, clues they figured out, map pieces retrieved, and adventures sneaking around. And now here they were by his side, skipping school because they believed his crazy story about the symbols and the map. These were truly two of the best friends anyone could hope for.

"Hey," said Josh. "Did you guys see the fourth member of our team today?"

"You mean Eli?" said Trip. "I saw him hiding in the bushes earlier."

"Well, this is it," said Sarah. "Are you guys ready?"

Trip looked again at Josh and Sarah. He was more ready than he could have imagined.

"Let's do this thing!" said Trip, and they walked down the road to finish the greatest adventure they may ever have.

Eli lurked along in the shadows, following their every move.


A large archway marked the entrance into the Fountain of Youth Park. It was the gateway to their adventure's conclusion. As they made their way through the archway and down the main path, the huge trees created an amazing canopy of branches. The dappled light made the whole place feel magical.

They stopped at a large statue of Ponce de Leon. It was here in this park, in April of 1513, that Ponce de Leon first came ashore in the New World and laid claim to the area for Spain, naming the place "La Florida" in honor of the *Feast of Flowers*.

And over three thousand years before that, the Native Timucua tribe prospered on this land. Trip thought about the Native American that had visited him in his dreams, and wondered if perhaps he was a Timucua. He swore he saw a fox stop and stare at him before scurrying off into the woods. He looked at Josh and Sarah, but they did not seem to notice anything.

As they approached the location of the original Fountain of Youth, the excitement mounted. Pappy had come here in hopes of finding the treasure, just as Trip did today. And long before that, Ponce de Leon was here drinking from the Fountain of Youth, believing in the legend that anyone who sipped its waters remained young forever.

Trip paused a moment and thought about what it must have been like for explorers coming to the new land. It must have been a truly mysterious experience. Looking at the foliage around him, Trip thought it was no wonder they thought the place had mystic powers.

They arrived at the original fountain and looked around. A small hole trickled water into something resembling a well, and statues depicted scenes of the Native Timucua interacting with the Spanish Conquistadores.

"This is it?" said Josh, disappointed. "This is the famous Fountain of Youth?"

"I guess so," said Sarah. "And this is where your dad and Pappy's trail ended."

"Yep," said Trip. "They thought the treasure was right around here somewhere. I wonder how long they spent looking?"

Trip opened his backpack and dug around inside.

"I know I packed those satellite maps in here somewhere. No worries, I know where we're going." Trip referred to a tourist map of the park. "OK, we're right here at the fountain. And we're trying to get here."

"Which means we should go that way," said Sarah as she pointed.

Josh didn't waist any time. He headed in the direction Sarah pointed.

"Time's a wasting," said Josh. "Come on, get the lead out, guys."

"That guy is like a roller coaster," said Sarah, and they chased after Josh.

Eli stepped out from behind one of the statues and followed.

Back at Trip's house, Mom was on the phone and stomped into Trip's room in a frenzy. She was talking with the school principal and could not believe what she was hearing. Trip was not in school.

"Yes, I'm sure he's not here at the house," said Mom. "I saw him leave for school this morning. I have no idea where he could have gone."

Mom started digging through his room. "Well, if you see him, will you please let me know? Thank you."

She hung up the phone and noticed some papers sticking out from between his mattress. She snatched up the papers and realized they were satellite images of what looked like the Fountain of Youth State Park. There was a red X in the middle of the park.

She grabbed the maps and blazed out of the house in a fury.

Trip, Josh, and Sarah were now on a small path with thick trees and bushes on both sides. They would need to go right through one of the thickest bunches of bushes.

"Are you kidding me?" said Josh. "You expect me to go through there? That could scratch me all up, and then I would have to explain to my mom where…"

Sarah barreled through the bushes without a word, followed by Trip.

"Oh, OK," said Josh. "I see how it's going to be."

Josh reluctantly followed. When they came out on the other side, they found themselves in a clearing. It was breathtaking. There were natural rock formations, and lush plants everywhere. The Florida aquifer bubbled up through the ground and created a small spring.

"All right," said Trip. "This is it."

"OK, what now?" asked Sarah.

"We need the book," said Trip. "We can't do anything else without the book."

"Are you sure this is gonna work?" asked Josh.

"There's only one way to find out," said Trip, and he yelled out into the woods. "Eli! We know you're out there. Come on out."

They waited for a few seconds, and nothing.

"Come on, Eli," continued Trip. "There's no need to hide. We know you're there. If you want us to find this treasure, we need that book. We can't do anything without it."

They waited a few more seconds. Trip was about to try again when Eli stepped out of the woods. He had the book in his hand, and he kept his distance.

"You're not getting this book back," said Eli.

"Without it," said Trip, "we all might as well go home."

"And guess what?" said Sarah. "We are not going home."

"Well it looks like we have a problem then, don't we?" said Eli.

At that moment, Trip hurled the cast iron plate at Eli's hand. It hit the mark, and knocked the book to the ground. Wasting no time, Eli rushed Trip. Sarah finally delivered the pepper spray she had promised right in his face. Eli went down in agony. Josh rushed over with some rope and tied Eli's hands.

"I didn't know treasure hunting was going to be such a yo-yo," said Josh. "It's boring, it's fun, it's boring, it's fun."

Josh made sure the rope was a little extra snug around Eli's wrists.

"And right now," continued Josh, "treasure hunting is really fun!"

"And now," said Josh, "treasure hunting is boring again."

Only a few minutes had passed, and Trip had spread out the four map pieces on the ground. He compared the symbols on the plate to those on the map. Josh sat on the large rocks playing on his portable game while guarding Eli. Sarah studied a page in the book that had some information about the symbols.

"According to this picture," said Sarah, "there's a knob or combination that we need. And it looks like it will open a gateway or passageway of some sort."

"What?" said Trip. "We're in the middle of the woods! There's no passage or gate here. We would see it."

"I'm not sure," said Sarah, studying the book again. "I could be wrong, but there are some references here to the Native Americans. Maybe they helped Gasparilla hide the treasure. I'm pretty sure the next step is to find a way to unlock the passage, and then we can figure out where the treasure is."

"Well, we're in the right place," said Trip. "I've looked over these symbols again, and it all adds up." Trip and Sarah looked around for anything unusual or out of place.

"Maybe the bushes or grass have grown over the entrance or something," said Josh.

"Josh, what are you working on over there anyway?" asked Sarah.

164

"I'm about to beat the level eight boss," said Josh. "He's tough, but if I can just..." He realized this was not what Sarah was talking about.

"Josh, we need your help," said Sarah. "Help us look for this thing."

Josh did not bother to get up. But he made a minimum, pathetic effort to look around.

"Well there's some water over there," said Josh. "And some rock over here, and some bushes..."

Josh stopped mid sentence when he noticed something on the rock right next to him.

"Wait a minute," Josh continued. "There's something in this rock. Look."

Trip and Sarah rushed over. A circular indentation was carved in the face of the rock.

"This is about the size of your Eli bashing plate," said Josh.

"It sure looks like it," said Trip.

Trip pulled out the plate. He took a deep breath and gently placed the plate into the indentation. It was a perfect match. The numbers on the plate started to glow with the soft golden light, just as he remembered from his dream. The plate became part of the rock, and a smooth circular crack formed around the rim of the plate. Another one formed around the inner circle of symbols on the plate. A soft light glowed from the cracks. The whole thing produced a complex dial. They gazed at it in awe.

"Cool, how's it doing that?" said Josh quietly.

Josh reached down and turned the outer circle of the plate. It rotated easily.

"What are you doing?" asked Trip, horrified. "Don't touch that until we know what we're dealing with! What happens if we do it wrong?"

"Stop worrying," said Josh. "This is just like the final level in Mysteries of the Temple Thief."

"A video game?" said Sarah, appalled. "This is not a video game, Josh."

"No, seriously," said Josh, still turning the dial. "It took me months to figure out how it worked. This is exactly like it."

Josh alternately turned the inner and outer dials. Each time he stopped and spun the dial another direction the sound of a giant rock pin sliding into place came from deep within the rock. Sarah and Trip exchanged an excited look. Josh engaged the final turn, and everything went silent. The plate separated from the rock and returned to normal. They stared at it in silence. Slowly, the sound of insects and birds returned.

"Aw, come on!" said Josh. "That was it! I know it was! Who programmed this thing anyway? That is so not fair."

Sarah tried to put the plate back in the rock indent. It did nothing.

"Josh!" said Sarah. "I told you not to mess with that until we knew what we were..."

Josh was not going to stand for this. "That was the right sequence! I know it was. If you would just give me a chance to..."

"Now we may never get to the entrance!" Sarah said fiercely. "You may have blown this thing!"

Suddenly the ground started to shake.

"Wait, guys," said Trip. "What's going on here?"

The ground shook more violently and a rumble could be heard from deep within the earth. Sarah grabbed Trip's arm and held tightly as the ground shook harder. The water in the spring next to them started to drain. Large pieces of rock crumbled inside the spring as the water disappeared.

Deep in a dark cave, ancient wooden gears turned and ancient wooden planks pushed through rock. Where there was once water, rocks pushed out of the walls and formed a crude stairway down into the hole.

Trip turned around and saw Eli backing away, terrified. He tripped over a rock.

"That's not right," said Eli, wide-eyed. "What are you guys doing? You're going to get us killed!"

Trip grabbed Eli and hoisted him up. He pushed him toward the stairs that spiraled down into the earth.

"The best way to conquer your fears," said Trip, "is head on. You lead the way."

Josh handed Sarah and Trip flashlights from his backpack. Trip pushed Eli ahead of him, and they descended the ancient stairway into depths unknown.

# CHAPTER TWENTY-SIX

They carefully worked their way down the spiral staircase and finally reached the bottom. Water dripped from above. There was a natural crack in the rock ahead. They barely fit through, but they shimmied their way through the narrow passage.

Eli was whining like a frightened six year old. "I want to go home. I want you to take me back to my mom right now."

"If you don't keep quiet," said Trip, "I'm going to leave you in here forever. Wait until everyone at school hears how brave you've been."

"I don't care," moaned Eli. "Tell them what you want. Just get me out of here!"

Trip kept pushing Eli along. The cramped tunnel opened into a small, square, man-made room. As they burst through, they spotted a weathered wooden chest sitting right in the middle of the room. Trip hurried to the chest and pushed Eli to the other side of it.

"Stay there," said Trip. "I'm watching you." Trip turned his attention to Josh and Sarah. "This is it! We found it!" His friends rushed over.

Shaking, Trip pulled a small pry bar from his backpack and with a little effort popped the latch off. Josh took a picture. This was the moment they had been waiting for. He held his breath as he slowly opened the chest. He peered inside, and found it was full of old Indian arrowheads and artifacts. He quickly dug through the chest and found nothing else.

"Are you kidding me?" said Trip, totally defeated. "It's just a bunch old arrowheads?"

"No," said Josh. "We must be missing something. This can't be all there is."

"No, Josh, face it," said Trip. "My Mom was right. This whole thing has been a waste of time."

"It doesn't have to be over," said Sarah. "We can keep looking. We'll go back to your house and regroup. I'll read through the book again and see if..."

"We've looked at the book," interrupted Trip. "We've followed the directions. We've opened the passage. And this is what was here. Maybe there was never anything here, or maybe someone else came here and took it already. Whatever it is, it's over. No more. I can't waste my life away like my dad and Pappy. And now Pappy is getting thrown out on the street, and we're going to get kicked out of our house."

Trip sat on the ground and buried his head in his hands. Eli took advantage of this moment, and broke into a sprint in an attempted escape. His foot caught a rock the size of a bowling ball and he lurched forward. He crashed into the rock wall, hard, with a dull, hollow thud.

"Did you hear that?" said Trip. "Did you guys hear that?"

Trip grabbed the stone Eli tripped over. He banged on the wall repeatedly with it. With each blow, there was a dull thud and rock crumbled to the ground. Josh grabbed a stone and started to pound on the wall too. Eli quietly worked his way towards the exit, still terrified. When he reached the opening in the wall, he shimmied through unnoticed.

They pounded on the wall, and the wall was breaking apart.

Mom was in the car with the pedal to the floorboard. She was completely flustered and had no idea what she was going to do to Trip when she got her hands on him.

Trip and Josh broke away a good portion of the wall, creating a door into darkness. Trip shined his flashlight around, and discovered a torch on the wall. He reached up, grabbing it, and found it was covered with spider webs. It was firmly attached to the wall.

"We need to light this," said Trip.

Sarah dug through her backpack and pulled out a lighter. She handed it to Trip, and he eagerly lit the torch. As the flame grew larger, it cast light across an ancient rope hanging directly above it. The rope ignited, and the flame quickly crawled up the rope into the newly discovered room. The flame raced higher and higher.

It reached its destination, high above. A huge ball of rope ignited, and the room was illuminated with the dancing light of the flames. All three friends were speechless, mouths hanging open in wonder.

There were life sized golden statues of Spanish Conquistadores, Timucua Natives, and pirates lining the walls of a room the size of a football field. Stairs crisscrossed the entire span of the four walls, reaching towards each other. They led down to the center of the room and created something that resembled an upside-down pyramid. Various chalices made of gold, diamonds, and rubies were scattered around on the stairs. There was treasure everywhere. Shiny jewels, necklaces, gold coins, and every type of treasure imaginable covered the room.

Where the stairs met at the bottom, a twenty feet long platform formed the focus of the room. In the center, there was a beautiful marble fountain about the size of a hot tub, with water flowing over its edges and draining into the floor below. Just beyond the pool was a simple chest made of wood.

"Now this is more like it," said Josh.

"It's amazing," said Trip.

Trip, Josh, and Sarah stepped over various artifacts, making their way to the center of the room. Trip and Sarah ran their fingers over the smooth fountain walls. The water was cool to the touch. Josh took picture after picture. Trip approached the wooden chest, and to his surprise, it was not locked. He took a deep breath, opened it, and looked inside.

It was full of the most beautiful pieces of the entire treasure room. Gasparilla must have kept his favorite pieces in this chest. Josh took a few more pictures.

"Wow, this really is beautiful," breathed Sarah.

"And it all belongs to me," said a dry old voice with a thick Spanish accent.

They were startled, and turned to see a pale, sickly man step from the shadows. The man looked tired, and his clothes were old and dirty. In his hand he held a walking stick, and perched on top of the stick was an ornately carved tree that twisted itself around into a perfect sphere. Nestled inside the tree was a wise old owl. The entire thing was carved from a single diamond.

Mom was inside the Fountain of Youth Park standing next to a large statue of Ponce deLeon. She referred to her map as

172

she tried to figure out which way to go. A clearly upset, disheveled boy came running past, crying and talking to himself. As he ran past, Mom swore she heard him say something about this park being cursed.

Was it possible the pirate Gasparilla himself stood in front of Trip, Josh, and Sarah? Gasparilla died about two hundred years ago. The man standing in front of them now was old and tired looking, but no one lived to be two hundred years old.

"My name is Gasparilla," said the man, in his tired Spanish accent. "How did you children find this place?"

"There is no way you are Gasparilla," said Trip. "Gasparilla tied himself to an anchor and flung himself into the Gulf of Mexico two hundred years ago."

"That is correct," said Gasparilla. "You know of me. I am impressed. I did tie myself to that anchor and throw myself into the Gulf of Mexico, just as you say. But now I am standing here in front of you, and I want to know how you found this place."

"My family," said Trip, clearly nervous. "My family has been looking for this place for a long time. We just used what they had already figured out."

"And how did you open the passage?" asked Gasparilla.

"We used this," said Trip, as he pulled out the cast iron plate.

Gasparilla took the plate from Trip. He studied it in silence for nearly a minute.

"This plate is mine," Gasparilla finally said. He almost seemed happy. "Clever children. I have been looking for this plate for a long time. I had the natives build me this place. But when they built the passage, they lost one of my plates."

Gasparilla went back to studying the plate intently. Josh snapped a picture.

"Look, whoever you are," said Sarah, "Gasparilla has been dead for a long time. Who are you really?"

"I am Gasparilla, the most feared pirate to ever sail the seven seas. The water that flows in that spring... People have been searching for it for centuries, but I am the one who found it. But in order for it to work, you need this."

Gasparilla held up his walking stick with the diamond tree.

"Are you saying this is really the Fountain of Youth?" blurted Josh. "The real Fountain of Youth?"

"Call it what you want, child," Gasparilla said. "But the water only keeps your body young, keeps you alive. The mind is not meant to stay alive this long. My mind is old, too old. I have gone insane down here. That is why I need this plate."

Gasparilla walked around the fountain, touching identical plates that were imbedded in the marble walls.

"This plate will rescue me from myself," said Gasparilla. "At first, all this treasure made me happy. I had to stay alive to guard it, protect it from thieves. It is my treasure, and no one else can have it. So I have stayed right here and guarded my treasure. For two hundred years, I guarded this treasure. Now you come and rescue me from my mind. I don't have to guard the treasure any more."

Gasparilla reached a spot in the fountain with an indentation, but no plate. He paused.

"I think we have a visitor."


At the top of the stairs stood Mom. She could not believe what she was seeing as she looked down into the massive treasure room.

174

"It's real," she whispered to herself. "I can't believe it's real."

"Please," said Gasparilla. His voice echoed up the stairs. "Come down."

Mom made her way down, still taking it all in.

"I was just telling these young people that I will no longer need to guard this treasure," said Gasparilla.

"Why?" asked Sarah, terrified to hear his answer. "Why don't you need to guard it anymore?"

"It's because you're giving it to us, right?" said Josh. "For bringing you that plate?"

Gasparilla placed the plate into the indentation and something rumbled in the distance. The plate glowed as it became part of the fountain.

"I will not longer need to guard the treasure," continued Gasparilla, "because there will be no more treasure. When my native friends built all of this for me, I had them create a way to destroy it if I ever needed to. And that is why I have been waiting for that plate. Now, I will be able to rest, the way we are meant to rest when our time on this planet is done."

He raised the diamond owl tree high above him. Right in front of their eyes, Gasparilla faded to dust, and a mysterious gust of wind carried him away. The walking stick fell to the ground with a clatter.

The rumble was much louder now, and the whole place shook violently. Rocks tumbled from the ceiling, the rumbling deafening. The fountain overflowed at an alarming pace, flooding the floor. The walls cracked. Gold statues toppled, and were crushed by giant boulders that fell from the ceiling.

"We've got to get out of here!" yelled Trip. "Let's go!"

Trip dragged Mom and Sarah up the staircase as it shook violently. He looked back and saw Josh, still taking pictures. Trip ran back to get him.

"What are you doing? Come on!"

He grabbed Josh and pulled him up the stairs. The entire room crumbled in a cloud of dust behind them.

At the top of the stairs in the arrowhead room, Sarah and Mom waited anxiously for Trip and Josh. Much to their relief, they emerged from the staircase, coughing but otherwise unharmed.

"This place is about to collapse!" yelled Mom. "We've got to get out of here!"

Trip took one last look into the treasure room and thought of what might have been. The entire roof of the treasure room collapsed with a deafening crash.

In the arrowhead room, a wall split as water broke through. Trip ran for it, and narrowly escaped being crushed as the arrowhead room was blasted away in a torrent of water.

Outside in the clearing, Sarah, Mom, Josh and Trip ran up the staircase into the open air. The stairs crumbled apart behind them as they ran. Smoke and dust billowed up from inside the hole. Just as they made it out, water exploded in a geyser from the hole. When it dissipated, the spring reformed, and everything settled down quickly.

Trip looked around, blinking. The place looked exactly the way it did before they opened the passage.

"That was amazing!" hooted Mom. "Did you see that place? I can't believe you guys found it. I can't believe it's real."

Mom grabbed Trip in a huge bear hug. Mom could not hide her happiness.

"I was so worried!" Mom said as she squeezed Trip tighter. "You're still grounded, you know? Oh guys, you are all so amazing!"

Mom grabbed Josh and Sarah and included them in the big hug. She held them tight and would not let go.

"Uh, Mrs. Montgomery?" said Josh. "You're crushing me!"

Mom still wouldn't let go.

"No, really," said Josh. "You're really hurting me. I think you're going to break something."

Mom let them all go, a little embarrassed. They all exchanged huge, triumphant smiles.

"Oh, yeah," said Josh, as he reached into his backpack. "Do you think anyone would be interested in this old thing?"

He pulled out the diamond owl tree. It still had a small piece of the broken cane attached to it. He also held a small pouch of coins and jewels. The group could not believe what they saw.

"When did you...? How...?" Trip tried to ask.

"I grabbed it and was trying to document the historic moment with a picture when you came back and manhandled me out of there. Why is your family so rough anyway?"

The group stared at Josh and burst out laughing.

"Oh, yeah," said Josh, opening the biggest pocket on his backpack. "You owe me some flashlights and rope and stuff. I dumped that stuff out in there to make room for this stuff."

Inside his backpack were handfuls of treasure from the wooden crate.

Josh looked at them all with a goofy smile. "What? Didn't you guys get any treasure?"

# CHAPTER TWENTY-SEVEN

Trip sat next to Pappy's bed, showing him pictures of the adventure. Josh really did take some wonderful shots.

"It was incredible, Pappy! And now everything is going to be fine," said Trip

"You are something else, Trip," said Pappy. "I knew you could do it. Thank you for giving this old man something to live for."

They shared a brief moment of pure, restful happiness. No treasure, no clues, no worries.

"Now, enough lolly-gagging," said Pappy. "It's time for you to get busy on that next clue."

"Next clue?" asked Trip. "What are you talking about? There are no more clues. We found Gasparilla's treasure!"

Pappy was full of pride and excitement. He looked deep into Trip's eyes. He wished he could take a drink from the Fountain of Youth so he could stick around to see what the future had in store for Trip.

"This is only the beginning, Trip," said Pappy. "You're going to do some amazing things."

He stared at Trip a moment longer and the intensity left Pappy's face.

"Now where is my neutron particle generator? Professor Pettigrew!" Pappy said. "Did you take my neutron generator again? You know I need it to travel back to my time."

Trip sat there, confused. Not by Pappy's delusions, but by what he had said in his moment of clarity.


Days later, Trip and Sarah walked hand in hand through the schoolyard as Josh caught up with them.

"Have you guys ever heard of PDA?" asked Josh, disgusted. "It stands for public display of affection, and it makes most people sick."

"Oh, get over it, Josh," huffed Sarah.

The trio approached Eli.

"Hello Eli," said Trip.

Eli jumped back. He was still a nervous wreck.

"Oh, hi, Trip," said Eli. "I was just... I was going to... Look, just leave me alone, OK? I just want to forget about this whole thing."

"Fine by me," said Trip. "Hey, did you see the front page of The New York Times today?"

Trip gave the paper to Eli. The cover donned a great picture Josh had taken of Trip in the treasure room. Trip read the headline.

"*Three teens make history with the archaeological find of the century.* Nice headline, don't you think?"

Josh leaned in and pointed at his credit for the photo.

"Look there," said Josh. "Photo by Josh Halover. That's me! I'm a professional photographer!"

"Hey, if we ever go on another adventure," said Trip, "we'll be sure to invite you along, Eli."

"Yeah? No, thanks," said Eli, as he tried to hand the paper back to Trip.

"You can keep that," said Trip. "Now I'm sorry we can't stay and chat, but 20/20 has us scheduled for an interview in twenty minutes."

Trip, Josh, and Sarah walked away. They could make things right with Eli later, but for now, it just felt good to rub it in.

## EPILOGUE

Trip, Josh, and Sarah stood in the middle of a beautiful field. The birds chirped happy tunes. The warm glow of the sun gave life to a beautiful green field surrounded by trees.

"I've got something I want to show you guys," said Josh.

Josh showed them the diamond owl tree.

"Yeah, we've seen that before," said Trip.

Josh twisted the broken piece of cane at the base of the tree.

"I know you've seen it, but have you seen this?"

The cane and the diamond owl tree separated to reveal a hidden compartment. Josh pulled out an ancient piece of rolled up paper.

"What is that?" Trip asked.

"Oh, it's just another map. That's all," Josh said, as he put the paper back into the compartment. He walked away, leaving Trip and Sarah with a million questions.

They chased after Josh, pressing him for details, but Josh wouldn't say a word.

An owl sat in a nearby tree and watched as Trip, Josh, and Sarah walked away into their future.

### THE END

# ABOUT THE AUTHOR

Scott Clements is a two time Emmy nominated sound mixer in the movie and television industry. After writing various movie scripts and the popular textbook "Production Sound, A Beginner's Guide to Equipment and Techniques", Scott turned his attention to writing his favorite type of book, children's fiction. His first book, "Gasparilla's Treasure" is an adaptation of one of his movie scripts.

Born in 1972, Scott grew up in Fort Walton Beach, Florida and currently lives in Orlando with his wife, son, dog, and three cats. Writing mostly late at night when there are less distractions, he enjoys using his laptop computer so he can have his four legged family members by his side.

## ACKNOWLEDGEMENTS

Nothing I do would be possible without the support of my amazing wife Paige. She is my strength. Without her, I could not even remember to bring my head with me when I leave the house.

And from my son Corey, I draw my inspiration and innocent view of the world. Without his belief that Daddy can do anything, I would not have been able to complete this book.

One final shout out to my big sister and editor, Enger Dickey. She stepped up when I was desperate for an editor, and was instrumental in bringing you this story.